Fear. Faith. Love.

The Golden Egg:
An Origin Story

T.D. Dickinson

Published by Franklin Publishers
Printed in the United States of America
For permissions, inquiries, or additional copies, contact:
Franklin Publishers
www.franklinpublishers.com

Dedication

I dedicate this book to the Creator of All, the Great I AM. To my Lord and Savior, who is the head of my life, I WANT TO THANK YOU! Without you, nothing is possible. Lord, it was you who was my trusted confidant in the midst of it ALL. Father God, it was your never-ending provisions that somehow always have made a way out of no way, and Lord, I thank you from the depths of my soul. For it was you who planted a seed in me, even before you placed me in my mother's womb and it was you that never left my side on this journey to cultivate this flower entitled Fear Faith Love. May this piece of literature bring nourishment to the soul to all those reading, feeding all those that are lost in the darkness with a direction to help them find their way back to the beginning, back to the light.

Disclaimer Notice

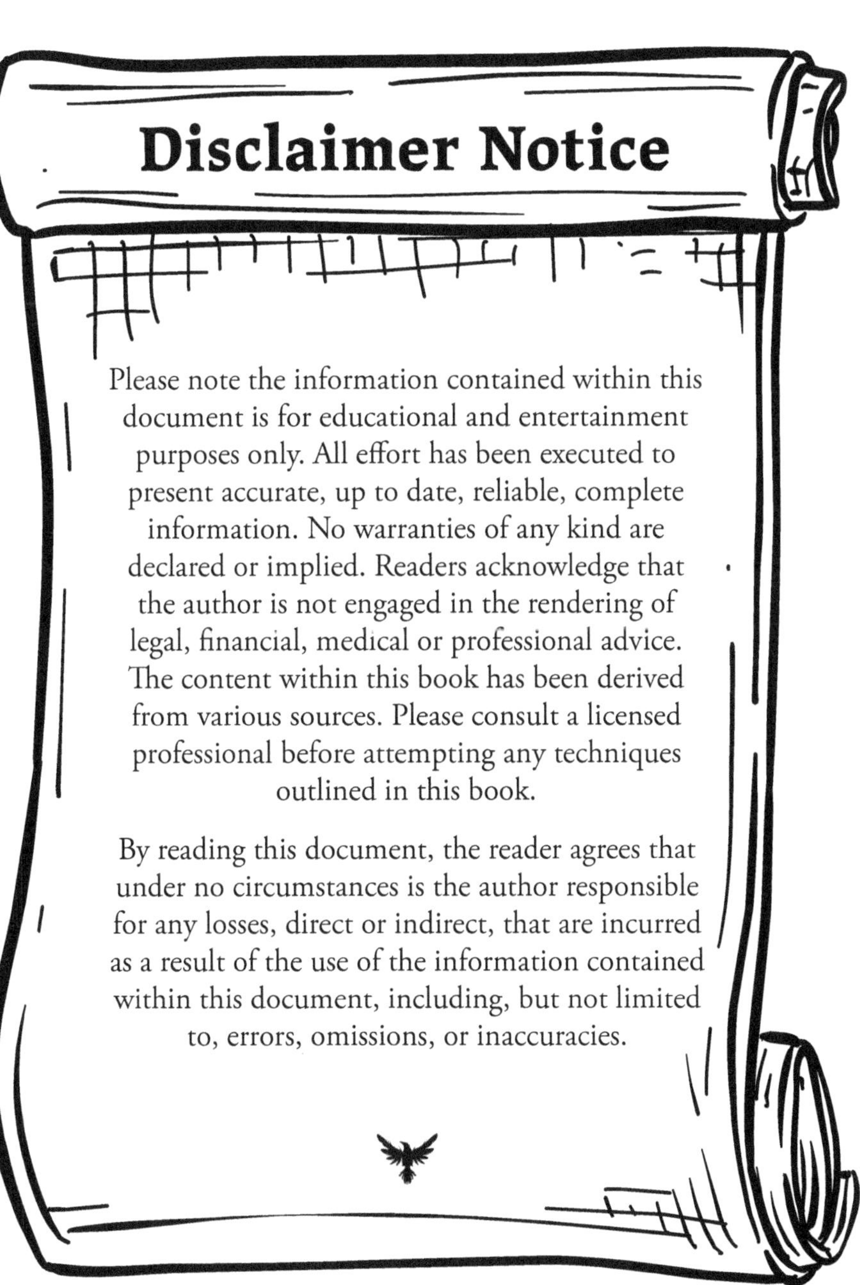

Please note the information contained within this document is for educational and entertainment purposes only. All effort has been executed to present accurate, up to date, reliable, complete information. No warranties of any kind are declared or implied. Readers acknowledge that the author is not engaged in the rendering of legal, financial, medical or professional advice. The content within this book has been derived from various sources. Please consult a licensed professional before attempting any techniques outlined in this book.

By reading this document, the reader agrees that under no circumstances is the author responsible for any losses, direct or indirect, that are incurred as a result of the use of the information contained within this document, including, but not limited to, errors, omissions, or inaccuracies.

Foreword

By Takeo Kingston

Bearing witness to my own Mom bringing her dreams to reality is almost a dream within itself. Mom, seeing you take control over your life—going from 400 lbs., sleeping all day—to living your biggest, wildest dream: fashion student by day, author by night, it is like you are a superhero.

Enough with the glaze, you are an amazing person and an even better Mom. I would not have anyone else.

Watching you create the FFL Saga was a lot. Most people do not know, but all throughout working on FFL, you have remained a light. That is why your art is so creative and beautiful.

During this process specifically, it has been more chaotic than most, yet you kept working on your craft, never ceasing. That is what makes me proud.

I am hoping to witness the birth of many more stories to come.

Love,

DooD

Preface

Every child has a dream. A dream of what their lives will look like, as an adult. My dream was not to be a doctor, lawyer, teacher, or even an entertainer, as most would like to think I would. My dream was, and still is, to be a mother.

I became a mother at the tender and impressionable age of eighteen. Shortly after becoming a mother, I became a young wife. As a young mother and wife, my then-husband and daughter accompanied me on many adventures. One of the largest was a tour in Japan at Yokota AB, where I was a meteorologist for the 20th OWS, US Air Force, Pacific Forces. While stationed in Japan, I gave birth to my second child, my first son.

Life got tough, and so did parenthood. I medically retired from the Air Force, and at an age not accustomed to retirement, there is where I found myself at 25. I had my third child, another son, after discharge. My children became my life after my not-so-traditional retirement. I was also simultaneously diagnosed with bipolar disorder. This diagnosis changed my life as my quality of life became dependent upon daily medications.

Over the next 15 years, I gained over 300 lbs., and I would embark on a journey with a destination of nowhere. Slowly, I sank into depression and became completely reliant on my mother. She dedicated her life to caring for my children and myself. I relied heavily on her support to help raise my children and I will forever be grateful.

When she was diagnosed with Glioblastoma Multiform, a form of Brain Cancer, I was filled with fear, fear of what the future held for my children and myself. My children and I spent the next few months caring for her, uprooting our lives, moving into her home to become our caregiver's caregiver. During this time, the pandemic hit, but we were already masked up and had hand sanitizer at every corner.

Mom died prematurely, just 10 months after her diagnosis. After the death of my mother, I sank into a very dark place. It was so dark that I began to push away all those whom I love. This included my dream, my children.

I went to dope to cope, not even mentioning the levels of desperation I sank to in searching for connection with anyone on this Earth except from the God-given connection I already had, my dream, my prayers, my children. I was in a place so dark that the only way out was either hell, jail, a mental ward, or to find spirituality.

I did not know which direction to go until someone came back into my life that sparked life and love into my spirit. This person woke up the creator in me that laid dormant for so many years. Love has a funny way of inspiring you to go within and find your true, most authentic self. Another funny thing about love is that you must be ready for it when it comes knocking at your door. If you are not, you run the risk of hurting each other, destined to becoming forever strangers who share beautiful memories.

Some call what we have a twin flame connection. Like all twin flames that have not healed, the fire of our love was extinguished; however, the spark of creativity continued to burn, refusing to die. With my children and the love of my life estranged, defeat was calling, and I was about to wave my white flag of concession.

But then, my brother Kerry asked me one day if I liked to write, and of course, I said yes. I had always been a reader, the child under a tree while all the other children would be running and playing. On January 8, 2022, I began drafting novels, and it came natural to me. The heart needs to ventilate, and it can only do that when we let out of us, what is bothering us on the inside. Writing has been my heart's ventilation system. Writing helped me heal, from the inside out.

As I began writing The Protection Squad: Vol 1, (a project I wrote, yet never published) I realized that not only being a mother was my dream but helping people through storytelling was also my dream.

As I began my fresh writing career, I was also in a full-blown episode of mania. I did not trust my surroundings and I was also very codependent on narcotics. Being from a small town with no relatives left was enough for the fear monster to creep in with all types of fears, such as squatters taking over my property, befriending the wrong people and trusting them, which could be detrimental to my freedom. I learned quickly that if you think it, it will be.

Very soon, my fears began to manifest, and I was no longer safe. People I had considered friends for years, I would call on, but no one would come to my nor my children's rescue. I did not know it then, but this was by divine planning. Through this pain, purpose was revealed.

So I packed up my car with just a few clothes and a pink guitar I swore to one day teach my daughter, leaving everything I was familiar with, children, inheritance, and all, and moved to St. Louis from little ole Mississippi (in my country accent) in May 2022.

This small-town girl had big city dreams, dreams so big, they prompted me to drop everything to pursue them. Following my dreams separated my children and myself, which is why I started writing Fear Faith Love. There were so many lessons I wanted them to know, and being apart from them for so long, I did what I knew to do best, and that was to write to them.

I knew that telling a story about the cycle of life needed to be interesting, so I used birds as muses as the characters. As a child, I was fascinated with all things birds. As a child, I was in the Talented and Gifted Program and in sixth grade, we studied all things birds at Carver Middle School. I became fascinated with all things birds.

I told my mother that I wanted to be a professional bird watcher, and she then took the time to inform me of the importance of financial security and the lack thereof that comes with such a profession. This is not to say that bird watching is not an honorable profession, this was just my mother's opinion at the time.

While developing, writing, and publishing the novel the first time around, I gave my life over to Christ and began to change everything about me. There is a saying that if you disappear for 6 months, you will come back a different person. Well, I did, and 13 months later we had the first attempt at Fear Faith Love.

I researched for months, everything birds. There are certain facts about the book that are taken from actual scientific facts. Stragif Strigiformes name and many of the main characters in this book are etymologized from their scientific classification. The scientific name for owls is Strigiformes, so Stragif, his wife Griphi, and daughters Phorma and Morpha are all from it.

Each character, and the special power that they bring to the story, are correlated with what the species naturally help with in our world. For example, owls are historically knowledgeable. This is partly due to how watchful they are. In the FFL Saga, owls are naturally the record keepers, historians, and educators of The Land. Eagles soar high and guard the mountains.

My biggest contributor in research of the cycle of life has been from God above. The Holy Bible has been my main source of reference for the cycle of life.

After publishing the novel, I learned a few valuable lessons:

1. You must kiss a few frogs before you find your prince.

2. Everything that glitters is not gold. There really is such a thing as fool's gold.

3. Be careful what you pray for because you just might get it.

4. Be ready to receive what God promises because He is a promise keeper.

5. The Lord blesses the truth, so stay in His presence. Stay in the light.

6. When you pray, detach from the outcome, going away knowing it will be done, on Earth as it is in Heaven. Whatever you think in your mind will become reality here on this Earth.

7. Comparison is the number 1 robber of joy. Minimize the opportunity to compare. Minimize social media exposure.

8. "If it ain't in the plan, it ain't gone land" The best way to manifest your goals is to set them, come up with a plan, and be like Nike and "Just Do It."

I have faced many hardships seeing this vision to life. In a world where we fear what we do not understand, those who dare to be themselves have been scrutinized for centuries. The writing, publishing, marketing, and publicity of this project has not been any different.

It is my prayer and my hope that through natural authenticity, this world begins to heal and live as one, just as the creator intended. It will not happen until we choose to not fear what we do not understand.

More than anything it is my prayer for all readers to take from it what you can and leave the rest for someone who needs it. Remember that there is nothing new under the sun. Whatever life brings you accept it as it is, expecting nothing, accepting only what is meant for you. Trying to understand such things as the "whys" of life is much like chasing the wind, utterly meaningless.

And without further ado, this is Fear. Faith. Love.

TD Dickinson

St. Louis, MO

Acknowledgments

To my children, Mx3, Mommy loves you to the moon and beyond.

Mekia (My Schoona Bug), may you reach your dreams and may they heal all those whom come in contact with them.

Malachi (My Halo from Heaven), may your sound harmonize the land, bringing love to the hearts of all who listen.

Matthias (My Dood, my JB), may your light continue to brighten the lives of all those whom it comes in contact with, never forgetting to replenish your own cup.

You three are the light of the world, so light it up. You three are the salt of the earth, may you forever bring the flavor and may we never lose it!!

To my mother, the late Mrs. Yolanda K. Jones (Yogi), I did it. I surrendered to Christ and now live in purpose. I love you; may you forever rest in eternal peace, for you are now with the Creator.

To my Daddy (Rev. Dwight E. Dickinson, Sr.), I love you!!! Your love and support has truly helped me transform. Your unconditional love has taught me what God's love is like. Agape Daddy! To be Shepherded by you is an honor and a privilege within itself. This is just another example of proof that God loves me.

To my grandparents, the late Rev. Dr. Richard C. Dickinson, Sr., his beautiful wife and my beloved granny, Ms. Blanche W. Dickinson, and the late Mr. and Mrs. Bennie and Henrietta King, whom we affectionately called Dada and MaDear—thank you for such a solid foundation in Christ. It is an honor to be a part of your lineage, and I wear it as a badge of honor.

To my stepparents, the late Mr. Kenneth Jones and the beautiful First Lady of Great Commission Lutheran Church, Mrs. Valerie Dickinson—thank you both for loving me as your own. You two have had a dynamic influence on my life that I hold near and dear to my heart. I love you both, now and forever.

To my uncle Bernard Dickinson, Sr., I love you. Thank you for always being down to show a girl a good time and spoiling your niece beyond words. Uncle, thank you for always knowing me for me. Next Cardinals game is on me.

A very warm thank you to my uncle, Mr. Kelvin D King (Uncle Boone). You bought my first keyboard for me at 3 years old and taught me "Kwinkle Kwinle, Little Star". I will never forget to shine Unc. I love you and thanks for ALWAYS being there for me and my mom. Thank you for never forgetting about me and always calling. We go on for hours in nostalgia, leaving the call better than when it started. Even in Mama's death, you are the ultimate big brother!

A special thank you to the congregation of Great Commission Lutheran Church. I love you all and thank you for each and every smile, every word of encouragement, every "attagirl," every "keep going!!"

A special I love you to the youth of my Sunday School class:

"Hey guys, no matter in life when you are reading this, NEVER GIVE UP! KEEP MOVING FORWARD. THE SUN COMES OUT AND BRIGHTENS THE DAY AFTER EVERY SINGLE DARK NIGHT! THAT IS A PROMISE."

Thank you to my literary agent, Sophie Brown and the whole team at Franklin Publishers. Your professionalism and knowledge of the industry was just what this project needed. You guys are truly a breath of fresh air.

An extremely special thank you to HGK. Thank you, Thank you, Thank you.

Thank you to Dr. Cindy Musterman, President of Stevens – The Institute for Business and Art, Dr. Emilee Schnefke, Academic Dean, and Lynn Wasson, Fashion Department Head. Going back to school in a creative field was intimidating at my age, yet the cohesive environment made way for my dreams to flourish.

Thank you to my fashion professor and Editor Advisor Magazine, AK Brown, for providing opportunities that are only dreamt of, such as being a part of a fashion photo shoot for Madison Rian's feature in Advisor Magazine.

A very special thank you to my brother, Mr. Kerry D. Dickinson, for never giving up on me, for always picking up the phone, for every prayer, every morning, for every minute you dedicated to my mental health and dreams, for being a great example of a Black Christian husband to Tasha, father to Kaiden, Karter, and Kamren, and most importantly, being my friend.

There is an old saying that in this life, you do not get to choose your family, but you do choose your friends. Magic happens when the title of family and friend becomes one. It was in the heart of this friendship that this book formed, and through story building and many nights of letting our imaginations run wild, our bond strengthened.

It is a real honor to be loved by you, brother. You are my Earth Angel brother. Thank you for never giving up. By the grace of God, you pulled me across the finish line to BECOMING!

This book was written as an outlet to safely express the imagination of the misunderstood. Kerry, thank you, and I love you, brother.

Table of Contents

Prologue

"Fear. Faith. Love. This is the true Cycle of Life," I spoke, the words etching themselves in the air, for they were the foundation of all things, after all. The burning red flames compromising the ceiling in the hall of stone that surrounded me provided warmth to my orange and brown feathers—a figment of blue flecking my tail. As a Rooster dedicated to the Golden Egg's protection, there was nothing else I could do but tell stories of elder days to what would one day hatch into this world full of livid things.

"All things that exist in the Universe are created with all the knowledge that there is to know," I continued, knowing the next set of words would contradict the very action I was currently doing.

"When one enters the realm of infancy, they enter the world with knowledge of it. All creatures learn to communicate as our elders, but in learning their language, the infant forgets everything they are wired to know." My words echoed in the empty rooms across Fort Gallus, my mind wondering if the unhatched egg could learn from them.

"As we learn a new way of life, we become fearful. This fear is replaced with the faith that our elders will protect us. That faith brings love along with it. For it is out of fear that we have the faith that love will save us all."

I felt a brief, chill air enter the room, and as I turned, through a long corridor of golden walls depicting the stories of the Creator, leading to the views of a vast sky, I saw Murdek, the moon, bringing the night and embracing the world below it in its cold winds. Tomorrow, Delmartica would bring warmth from the sky to us once again. After all, that was the duty of the Sun.

"Have I ever told you the story of Raven, little one?" I asked, turning to face the Golden Egg once more. Its gilded surface reflected the moving flames above us, with a hue of gold beaming out of it. To be near something that came from the very Sun itself was, indeed, incredible; the structures I set my feet atop shockingly did not melt under such a powerful presence. The Egg represented the day itself, locked inside a fortress of ave-made stones.

"Raven was a god like no other Ave, for its story was filled with fear. From Murdek, he allowed his curiosity to take the best of him, putting himself on a path as close to madness as the tales of old ages remind us. In a world as vast as this, anything is possible. Yes, it's even possible for a young god to yield to temptation."

With my chest and comb proudly held high, I walked through the halls leading to the outer layers of Fort Gallus, stopping halfway through. No matter how many times I would look at them, the pictures depicting the history of creation and the Order of the Aves were magnificent. And then, another chill wind passed by me—this time, not made by the night announcing its arrival but by my own mind staring at the horrors of the Dark Years of Madness.

"Oh, little one," I began, returning to the Golden Egg's presence. "The vastness of this world allows for so much to happen. As you're yet to be born, you might already know of it, but please, entertain this lonely Rooster, will you?"

I briefly paused for a moment, expecting the egg to answer, though I also knew he would never do that.

"Thank you for humoring me," I elected to myself. "I expect Raven's story to soon be inscribed in the Halls of Memory leading to your chamber, as the days he spent on the Land were just as terrible as the days the Aves endured during the Dark Years of Madness. Back then, the Orders of Aves conjured by the Creator—each to execute a function of their own—multiplied faster than the Land itself could provide them with sustenance, leading to suffering never experienced before. Treachery and doubt rose from such dark times, and the Order of the Corves's decision to ally with the Family of the Crows and the Family of the Gaizers was unprecedented in the history of creation. If not for the intervention of the Phoenixes, the Land would've dried."

I walked close enough to the Hallway to spot a drawing from a more recent event, where five eggs were brought to Mount Kingdom Come; a sad day that one was—a ramification that sprouted from the years of darkness, a consequence unforeseen only met in the future. Most people are still unaware of this tale.

"Consequences are something I might have to teach you as soon as you reach the age of flight. There is nothing worse than not knowing the meaning of an act and the repercussions it causes. Not even Sunshine and Starlight can escape the consequences of an action. Only the Creator might."

I turned my back towards the little one, piercing my gaze through the Hall of Memories where the night sky could be seen touching the Land and the farm of crops me and my kind kindly took care of.

"It's due to consequences that I'm here, little one." But, of course, the Golden Egg had nothing to add. Instead, it towered over me. "Let's hope the mistakes that almost brought the Exodus before never come to pass once again."

I felt the warmth of the Sun's core touching my feathers, as in the Golden Egg's presence, it was inescapable. The aureate rays of light reflected from the Golden Egg and moved across the Hallway of Memories.

"Fear. Faith. Love," I proudly whispered to no one but myself, aware that soon, I would have to welcome another day in the Land.

At all costs, I would protect the Golden Egg of the JuJuRana, as the Phoenix, Sunshine, and her partner, Dwighticus, entrusted me. The duty of an Order of Aves has to be executed in perfection, and this is mine.

Fear. Faith. Love.
This is the true cycle of life.
All things that exist in the universe, are created
with all knowledge there is to know. When one
enters into the realm of infancy, one enters the
world with all knowledge of it. We learn to
communicate as our elders, but in learning their
language, we forget everything we are wired to
know. As we learn a new way of life, we become
fearful. This fear is replaced with the faith that
our elders will protect us. That faith brings love
along with it, for it is out of fear that we have the
faith that Love will save us all.

In a world as vast and as big as ours,
it is hard to comprehend just how
amazing our universe is.

TO UNDERSTAND,
ONE MUST GO BACK
TO THE BEGINNING.

CHAPTER I

The Loneliness of the Fall

As the sun's daily shift came to an end, the moon assumed its rightful position in the sky, bringing with it the night for the Land. Atop a cliff on the moon stood Raven against silver rock and sand, his plumage sharing the same hue as the soil of the moon, if not slightly brighter.

Distant to the west was the sun, and as it retired for what we know as nightfall, its rays illuminated a part of the land, creating a perfect division of day and night—one perpetually chasing the other, ever-changing their reach of the Land, never to meet just as the Creator intended.

"Why do you hesitate? This isn't your first time," the large Silver Phoenix spoke, flying far above the surface of the moon. Her plumage mirrored Raven's, yet her knowledge and wisdom yielded her two majestic silver halos that adorned the crown of her head.

"Will it hurt if I fall again?" Raven asked, staring at the bottom of the cliff from its edge.

"You are Master of the Winds. They were created to bow at your command. Now, command them, young God, and you shall not fall again," the great Silver Phoenix spoke with reverence. "It was your curiosity that led to such a little incident. Now come to me."

"Understood, Starlight," Raven replied, his voice full of uncertainty.

Raven approached the edge of the cliff, he clasped his wings together, keeping them as close as possible to himself, giving him the singular shape of a rock. Filled with the faith that Starlight would protect him, Raven jumped.

As Raven fell—his gray beak pointing downwards—his speed increased dramatically. The wind moved on its own, surrounding the young JuJuRae, and seconds before coming beak to sand, Raven spread his wings, allowing the wind to lift him, just as he had commanded. For the first time, Raven was flying, hovering just above the moon's surface, seeing it pass underneath him faster than his eyes could keep track of.

Raven flapped his wings once more, and the wind moved underneath them, propelling him upwards. He felt weightless, reaching ever higher. And the higher he went, the closer to the stars he became. There was something about them that mesmerized him; they twinkled much like the sun, but from so distant, their light emanated; they shaped themselves like singular dots of white painted across the dark fabrics of the void.

"You made a promise," Raven heard coming from just below. He hadn't noticed, but he had surpassed Starlight's altitude.

"My apologies," the young god replied, returning to Starlight's side. "My only intention was to see how far I could fly with the least amount of wind possible, I swear!"

"I've lived long enough to understand one's intentions, and only the dishonest end an explanation with a swear." Starlight reprimanded.

"In due time, you shall learn more about the stars. You just barely entered your age of flight. Those secrets would be far too much for one that just left their infancy."

"I understand," the young one replied as his mind took him back to his previous flight—to the second he came too close to a star. So bright was its body he couldn't see, leading him to enter a spiral downfall towards the moon. This experience he would never forget.

"Let's go, youngling," Starlight began, "Delmartica's blessed light will soon partially reach this section of the moon."

"Why can I not touch the light of the sun?"

"We are gods of the night. We watch over all that is cold, dark— over wind and hydra. The pleasures of the sun's warmth, for beings of our kind and power, would cause only pain."

But this darkness seems so sad, Raven thought to himself.

"But don't fret, youngling. Murdek waits for us."

"What if I choose to touch the sunlight just a little bit?" Raven questioned.

"Then, just like you once tried to briefly touch a star, a consequence shall be faced. And I need not repeat myself on those matters. Some consequences are far beyond even my power to amend."

But we are gods, Raven thought as he flew back to Murdek. His eyes never looked forward but, instead, upwards—to the tapestry of existence and its bright, little charming dots. He barely needed to move his wings; the wind itself would carry him home.

Murdek was—and still is—a giant oasis at the center of the moon. Hydra filled the oasis, while the winds brought a constant breeze that cooled down the rare days Murdek was faced directly by the rays of the sun. Lines of trees surrounding the lake, as well as mountains made with a gray stone whose surface shone as if it was actually a metal, created opportunities for Raven to hide in shadows from the sun's almighty flaming light.

Raven didn't quite know what would happen if such an event were to occur, but Starlight had been adamant about avoiding sunlight just as much as she had been insistent that the stars were to be left alone.

While Starlight rested on a pole near the center of Murdek, Raven moved about the remains of the egg from which he hatched. The shells were of a silvery smoke color, and they were far larger than the eggs that had to be hatched by the Aves of the Land.

"Have you heard anything from Delmartica?" Raven inquired.

"When the Creator deems it to be, so it'll be. Until then, the Golden Egg shall remain safely in the care of my sister, the Golden Phoenix, Sunshine," Starlight replied. "Because everything that exists has a function, you must master why you're here, young one. We are the protectors of the night; the JuJuRana are to protect the day. On the Land, the Aves possess their own Orders, each designed by the Creator to sustain the world," Starlight answered in a calm manner, much like a mother telling a bedtime story to her little hatchlings.

"And what about the Stars, are they—" But a strong surge in the wind prevented him from finishing the sentence.

"Do I need to repeat myself?" said Starlight, her voice bending the will of the wind as her own. "You made a promise to ignore the stars for the time being."

"Apologies," little Raven said as he hopped inside the lake's hydra to hide his frustration.

As he cleared his plumage of the moon's dust, he noticed the hydra reflected the stars above. He felt so close to them. As he touched the hydra, the wAves he created distorted the reflection, and they escaped from his grasp.

Why? Raven cried inside himself. *If I'm a god, why are there things I should not know about? Yes! I'm a god. I should not be held back from my own curiosity!*

Raven took flight, leaving the oasis of Murdek behind.

"I'll just fly to dry my feathers faster!" he screamed, hoping Starlight would just observe.

Raven did not stop. He continued higher and higher, and the stars kept getting closer and closer. He felt the winds briefly ignoring him, but with a single flap of his silver wings, they obeyed his command and pushed him ever higher.

There he was, face to face with a forbidden star. Murdek seemed distant. Delmartica remained hidden inside the sun, and the Land stood still, surrounded by the magnificent blanket of the darkness void, interspaced by the white dots of light.

He extended his wings, approaching the light, feeling the energy emanating from it, humming as if it were telling him a story of secrecy.

But I made a promise, he thought with guilt, quickly refraining from touching it.

He took the wind from underneath his wings and allowed himself to slowly begin his descent back home.

No matter how close he moved towards Murdek, Raven noticed that the hum of energy remained constant, as if he had never left the star's side.

And then, the hum grew louder. He felt light itself approaching him. He turned backward, witnessing the star following him, approaching faster than he could descend.

In the blink of an eye, they were one.

Light covered all existence in a flash that shook all that there is. Raven lost control of his body, feeling the acceleration of a fall he could not avert as his wings burned with fumes of pure white energy. The moon briefly passed in front of his eyes, and instead of landing on it, he kept on falling, noticing, for a brief second, Starlight crying.

The fumes of white soon began to trace all colors of the spectrum, creating a rainbow of smoke.

Raven fell for what seemed an eternity, and suddenly, another flash of light covered the Land.

The ground felt different than the usual arid and rocky silver sands of the moon. It was rocky for certain, but it was also grassy, itchy, and strangely enough, humid. When Raven came to his senses, his surroundings were embraced by the night. But this was not akin to the eternal night witnessed from home. No, the one surrounding him was far darker and colder.

"Woo. Woo," he heard, the sound coming from beyond the trees around the crater created by his fall's impact. If any fire was formed, the flames had been put out by the passage of time and wind. The only proof of its existence was the darkest smoke that rose from the circular charred ground.

Strangely, the exact location where Raven fell remained intact, the green grass now covered by the shadows of the trees—their creation coming not from the light of Delmartica but instead from the silver shine of Murdek.

Murdek! exploded Raven in despair, staring at the sky, his gaze attempting to pierce beyond the foliage crown of the trees and into the sky above, but the attempt failed.

Raven flapped his dark silver wings, commanding the wind to sustain his body and lift him upwards, but the wind didn't respond in its full glory; it just marginally moved around, surrounding his wings.

"Woo. Woo," echoed across the forest once again, chilling Raven so deeply he felt he had lost all of his feathers.

What is this feeling? He asked himself.

"Woo. Woo," he heard once again, this time coming from a different direction.

"Starlight?" Raven whispered in silence.

It can only be her. She is the only person I know… She is… the only one, but his thoughts slowly succumbed to a feeling that he'd never felt before as he came to terms with not being under Starlight's domain anymore.

Raven flapped his wings, overwhelmed by something new and strange. The gust moved in every direction, becoming chaos incarnate. The smoke got carried away, the leAves fell from their branches and flew under a music without rhythm, and the young god's immense wings finally managed to get a hold of themselves and lift him upwards.

On the way up, he crashed against multiple branches, each hit flashing a memory from Starlight telling him what to do and what he should never do. This time, he'd done the latter.

Beyond the destroyed foliage stood an enormous, dark sky. The stars remained in the same positions he was used to seeing them, but that was all he could recognize. Across the horizon stood large stretches of land covered by tall trees, a sea of green on green; all that the eye could see was indistinguishable and featureless but for a lake fed by a river coming from the snowy mountains in the east.

And shining above it all, brighter than even the stars, stood the moon.

I'm on the Land, Raven told himself, his eyes widening as his home seemed like a silver dot moving across the skies. *I'm on the Land…*

Raven closed his eyes, trying to summon the winds to follow him, but they never came. His mind moved back in time to Starlight's lesson before his first flight attempt.

The winds obey me, for I am a god, but for Aves of the Land, they have to tame it.

He flapped his wings, moving not at random but as the wind moved, pulling and pushing just as Starlight taught him before.

For every movement of his wings pulling him ever upwards, the further Murdek seemed to get. The space in between the Land and Murdek was the emptiest thing Raven had ever seen. Even the stars were closer to the moon than the sky itself.

The higher he flew, the colder it became. Eventually, the air grew rarer, and so did his awareness. Raven felt dreadfully tired, having difficulty sustaining himself afloat for much longer.

Soon, there was more air on the surface of the moon than there was in the void between the Land and the rest of creation. His feathers became stiff—frozen in place, making every maneuver harder to execute. Suddenly, the air vanished, and for the second time in a short period, Raven found himself falling without any control.

The ground didn't receive him as kindly as when first fell. This time, the hit was hard, and cracks sprung from the area around him.

"Woo. Woo," cried towards him once again—this time, further deep into the forest.

When Raven searched for the source of the noise, two immense yellow eyes stared at him from afar. Once again, the same strange feeling overcame him, his heart beating faster and faster.

What is this that I feel? he wondered. *No! You won't get me, creature! You won't!*

Raven ran before flying, gaining altitude slower than he would've liked, only to find himself falling down once more.

During hot days, when the air is warm, it would create upward currents one could easily glide on, he recalled Starlight teachings.

And more.

During the cold nights, the winds would stay still, falling down dormant over the Land, Starlight once mentioned in a lesson on the way of the Aves of the Land, where the wind was not their own to command.

He fell again.

And in between, the transition of up and downward currents, as a day's weather, is never constant. The air would move left and right, according to the change in weather, creating pockets of movement for your wings to ride.

And again.

Repeating his chase for the moon, Raven tried desperately to find the winds that would carry him home. He ran fast while evading the eyes of his pursuer, just to have Murdek evade him even more.

Eventually, red beams of light painted the horizon from beyond the eastern peaks as Murdek vanished to the west inside the vast green sea.

When Raven touched the ground again, he didn't know how many times he had tried. The only certainty that he had was that he had failed—that his feathers were frozen, his body and bones were broken from each consecutive fall, and the dirt of the soil surrounded every inch of his body as if it owned him.

Where once was a forest with no distinctive features, now a clearing filled with craters had taken its place.

The light of Delmartica encroached on the Land slowly. *The sunlight will touch me,* cried Raven to himself, trying to muster the force to move out of the clearing, reaching for the shade of a tree. But he couldn't move. He just couldn't.

"Woo. Woo," he heard once again—this time, incredibly close. He gazed to the place where the voice came from, a section of the forest still claimed by the light, and there it was, those terrifying yellow eyes gazing back at him.

"Woo. Woo," the creature gently pronounced as it left the confines of the shadow. The ave itself was half Raven's size, filled with gray feathers all around, interspersed with white feathers at its chest and neck.

"Who are you, woo? Who indeed?" the creature spoke softly. Its head was almost as large as its body.

"I'm Raven, I'm a—" But Raven couldn't finish his sentence, for his bruises gave him much pain.

"Raven, woo? You seem different from any Order or Family I have ever seen," the ave replied. "You fell like a rainbow from the skies, woo. Magnificent it was! A Delmartican, I imagine?"

"No," Raven replied, conjuring enough energy to speak. "I'm from—" But before the sentence could be concluded, the ever-encroaching sunlight filled the crater, touching Raven's feathers and creating abundant light—light that sprung from the myriad of flames, each consuming one of Raven's feathers.

"No, this can't—" Raven screamed, but from inside his beak, black smoke rushed out.

"To the hydra, woo. There is a lake nearby," quickly pointed out the ave.

Raven once again mustered the energy required to move around and ran towards the lake.

He fell inside it, and to his surprise, the flames didn't vanish.

"By the Creator's holy plumage! You appear to be on fire still!" exclaimed the gentle ave, adjusting the glasses on top of his beak. "Follow me, woo!"

The creature flew above Raven, guiding him to a section of the lake covered by the shade of the encompassing forest.

As soon as Raven's body escaped the sunlight, the flames were put out.

And as soon as a little piece of sunlight moved between the space created by the leAves, he would completely burn once more.

"It's the sun," Raven exclaimed to the intriguing ave, remembering how Starlight was adamant about telling him of the dangers of just having a single tip of his feather coming in contact with it.

"Maybe deeper, woo?" questioned the mysterious ave, guiding Raven to the depths of the forest.

But Raven's body was far too large for him to be completely covered by the trees, and just like his attempt at the lake's margin, the treachery of the sunlight and its ability to move between spaces set him aflame once more.

And it was painful. His feathers might not be truly burning, but his skin underneath them was.

Finally, Raven noticed a cave nearby, connected to a section of rocks extending from the mountainside.

He rushed inside the place, hoping it would finally do the trick. At first, the light from his flames illuminated the cave walls, revealing all the moss around him. The creatures living inside rushed out in fear.

Seconds later, the cave returned to its original color palette: pure black.

"It worked, woo!" The stranger celebrated from afar. Seconds later, he fell silent, watching the sky above. His gaze immediately returned to Raven's feathers. He stared at its dark silver colors for far too long, deep in thought. Somehow, he could distinctly see inside the cave.

"Raven, correct?" the bird started once again. "I hope you forgive me, but as an Owl, my duty is bound to the night. I'm afraid I must leave."

"No, please. There is—" But before Raven could finish his sentence, the owl was already far too distant for him to reach.

Raven passed the following days and nights in solitude. During the day, he would spend all his time by himself deep in the belly of the cave, where no light could ever dream to reach him. Once the night greeted the land, Raven would attempt to fly ever higher towards Murdek, failing every single time.

The forest beyond the lake region seemed alive. Sounds of the foliage moving, branches breaking, and birds chirping and singing echoed across the day, and in the night, the Owls would make the place their own.

The creatures that once lived in the cave approached it later, but as soon as the silhouette left by Raven's enormous body met their eyes, they ran away, never to return.

From time to time, the strange feeling that Raven had felt the moment he noticed he was on the Land would return to him, giving him shivers even when it wasn't cold.

As the Creator ordained, the night had fallen once more. The forest had grown silent, the sound of the Owls doing their diligent duty had become commonplace in Raven's ears to the point where they were not even there.

Another round of attempts to reach Murdek ensued. Another series of failures emerged.

Eventually, Raven did the usual and flew down, letting himself float above the calm lake—the fresh hydra so still, it created a mirror for the sky.

"Woo. Woo," Raven heard approaching. But when he turned to see its source, no one came to his side.

Murdek and the stars were present inside the hydra, reflected just like the stars once were reflected by the oasis in Murdek. No different from the oasis there, no matter how many times Raven tried to reach it, the reflection would not be touched, escaping from him as it slowly dissipated with the turbulence he caused with every movement.

Unlike other evenings, clouds gathered in the sky, blocking the view of the void beyond, hiding Murdek from sight.

It was the first time Raven felt the rain.

Chapter 2

The Monster in the Night

The morning dew settled across Raven's feathers, even in the depths of the cavern. The rain had filled the crater left by Raven's fall, transforming it into a small lake.

The fresh hydra grew stronger from the river's nascent flow, and the once-calm lake—that served so well to give Raven as much proximity as he needed—was now a turbulent storm.

Daylight prevented Raven from engaging in most of the day's activities, so the neophyte of the Land spent most of the time sleeping, preparing for the long nights of failed flight attempts, and hunting down his next meal.

For the first time since his birth, Raven felt the pain of hunger and the pain of hunting down his own food. Back on Murdek, the Creator would provide Starlight and himself with all he ever needed.

But Raven wasn't the only one afflicted by the morning dew. Carved inside the trunk of a hollow tree, a small family went about their morning business, preparing for a whole day of sleep, allowing the night to be their playground—the time when their duty would be fulfilled.

"Let me see your writing," asked one of the owls—the same one that visited Raven so many nights ago.

The youngest of the hatchlings, with silver and gray feathers, was wearing a tiny brown ribbon on her head. She took a notebook out of a dark yellow cloth that resembled a little bag.

"Here it is, Daddy," the young hatchling said, presenting him with the notebook. The large owl adjusted his glasses and quickly glanced across multiple pages of work.

"It's strange to see my own name written in a book like a record," he proudly proclaimed, "but I quite like the sound that comes out of it. Maybe I should call myself 'Stragif, the Rainbow Hunter' as you mentioned here, Morpha."

"What scholar will I be if I can't record the things I see?" Morpha questioned.

"The trick," began Stragif, "is to not record what you see but the reality of something. By giving me a nickname, you embellished the story beyond reality."

"But you did hunt the mysterious ave that fell with the rainbow," the older sibling replied. Unlike her sister, she had her gray feathers interspaced with brown ones. Around her neck, a red scarf created a distinctive look, contrasting with the soft yet round black glasses she was wearing.

"I paid him a visit, yes," Stragif mentioned.

"A single visit? Singular, just one? Once?" the older one questioned. "I swear, you go watch him every night."

"I bet you think he is the Stranger. That is the only explanation, Phorma," Morpha quickly added.

"Oh, the monster. Dad did mention the rainbow bird had dark feathers," Phorma continued.

"Calm down, hatchlings," said a tall woman preparing a meal for them. "Did I not tell you to never go about calling other Aves monsters? It matters not whether they are dangerous. They are still part of creation. The Stranger is a far more intriguing name, don't you think?"

"Sorry, Mom," the two girls replied in unison.

"I paid him more than one visit," Stragif replied with watchful eyes over Phorma. "I had to compare his features to all the features in the books about the Order of the Aves. I had no success. He is mysterious indeed, but also…"

"Also?" The girls questioned him together, eager to hear an answer.

"Sad, my girl. Woo. Something about him brings me so much sadness. His watchful gaze over the sky is terrible for us all."

The girls' faces broke down in disappointment. "Should we leave the forest?" Stragif's wife, Griphi, asked. "There are multiple places an Owl can be. The courts of a king would delight me much."

"We can do that for sure, woo," Stragif mentioned, "but they don't accept every owl that comes around. We need to train the girls to do their diligent duty. Then, we can find a better place to live."

"So, we need to record more in our books, Dad. More and more," Morpha said.

"We do, indeed. We shall go out tonight to add more to your books. Phorma already has one fully written," Stragif said.

"Are you hearing that, my little hatchlings? Your father is giving the two of you another chance," their mother said.

"Yes, Dad. We promise to follow your orders this time," Morpha adds.

"Indeed, Father. We won't rush towards the rainbow of light like we did last time. We promise," Phorma added.

"And I shall take you upon your words," Stragif said in a parental tone.

In the darkness that befell the Land that same day, Stragif departed to his duty of watching the events of the night, recording all that happened while others slept—their secrets exposed without protection of their minds. Phorma and Morpha accompanied him for the first few hours, as usual, before splitting to their designated area—the two girls sticking together.

"Did you read it?" Morpha asked in hushed whispers, making sure her father wasn't around to listen.

"Yes," Phorma replied in the same tone of voice. "Dad's book mentions that the bird spends his days inside the cAves."

"Are you sure about this?" Morpha questions.

"Of course I am! If we record a unique bird that fell from the sky in a rainbow, there will be no place in the world where our family won't be accepted."

The two quickly moved away from their post and followed their instincts towards the mountains, clinging to the riverside as most of the hydra passed by the cAves where it entered the forest. Soon, the two girls found their mark.

They slowly entered the cave. Due to the recent rain, the humidity had taken full control. As Phorma described the surroundings to her younger sister, Morpha wrote every word, cataloging the place.

Suddenly, they heard something cracking under their feet. When they took a look at it, they saw a pile of white objects.

"For the eating habits of the rainbow bird," Phorma described, "note that there are strange rocks shaped in horizontal patterns, resembling… bones? Yes, it resembles small bird bones."

"A predator, huh?" Morpha added.

The moon's silver light coming from the cave's entrance suddenly vanished. As with every Owl, they could see in the dark, but the abrupt change in the cave's lighting made the girls' hearts skip a beat.

Far down, from the darkness of the cave, came a song. Something was singing, but what it was, the girl couldn't discern. Carried by the winds, objects from beyond the depth move towards them: piles and more piles of bones in different sizes from Aves and other animals.

"I think… We better go now," Phorma said, turning back to the cave's entrance.

They screamed with the sudden realization that what had covered the moon's light wasn't a cloud or a tree but a giant dark being towering over them.

"Yes," the mysterious bird said maniacally. "Scream, little ones, bring more towards us for, tonight, I shall have dinner in abundance!"

Stragif stood by the lake, watching over Raven, documenting his attempts to catch food. They were not very successful. The worms and fish would quickly vanish from his grasp faster than he could flap his wings.

Hunting habits are still clumsy, but he is evolving at it, Stragif recorded in his mind to pass on to a book later.

A scream echoed across the forest from two voices far away, and they were very similar to voices Stragif knew far too well.

But it *couldn't* be his girls. The sound came from a completely different direction than their assigned post. Still, Stragif did as any father would and flew as fast as he could to his daughters' post to confirm that they were there.

His heart sank when he was met with their absence. The only person there was his wife. "Tell me they are with you…" she said in despair.

"They will be. I'll go towards the screams. You search the vicinity here. Don't follow me."

Stragif soared above the river, following the screams' general direction. He soon found a series of cAves. At one of the entrances, a small brown ribbon flew with the wind, unable to move any distance as it was attached to a little stick.

The girls are so smart. They at least marked where they went for me.

Stragif walked inside the cave, feeling the humidity rising and a strange voice singing deep in the depths.

Then, the singing was no more, as Stragif felt a blunt force to his head and collapsed to the ground.

"That's it? No mommy?" the Stranger said.

To fight the cold and humidity, the owl family remained trapped in a tight embrace.

"Sorry, Dad," the girls said in unison, both crying. "We made a promise, and we broke it… And now… Now…"

"*Scream!*" screamed the bird. "Call for your mommy. I'm hungrier than you think."

"We won't—" Before Stragif could finish the sentence, he was smacked in the face.

"*Scream!*" the Stranger yelled again, hitting him in the face once more.

Stragif let the girls go and stood tall in front of them. "It'll be alright," he told them. Somehow, he believed in those words. "The Creator will protect us from all evil."

Something in those words triggered the mysterious bird.

"All of my prey called for the Creator. None survived," he said, his tone shifting wildly. Now… *Scream!*" he shouted, throwing multiple punches at Stragif, his wings far larger than the owl that seemed so little in comparison.

Then, Stragif caught his wings. "Fly, girls," he shouted. "Don't look back!"

The girls rushed out of the cave, obeying their parent as one should.

The mysterious bird shoved Stragif against a wall. The impact made him let go of his grip.

Suddenly, the silver moonlight vanished, drawing the cavern silhouettes into pure darkness.

"Mommy, you finally arrived—" A gust of air flew from the entrance, manipulated by the creature standing there. "What creature deems it prudent to hurt *me*?"

"One who does not dare to insult the Creator," Raven said, moving forward into the cave, allowing the light to move in and reveal his deep silver feathers. The darkness belonged to him, the night was his own, and he wore it well. Behind him, the two girls were flying as distant as they could.

"Another crazy one. Well, looks like dinner tonight will be incredible."

The Stranger rushed towards Raven, shoving him out of the cavern in a surprisingly majestic soar for something so immense. And for something so immense, it quickly hid in the shadows of the trees. Raven took flight, trying to scan the area from above, but all he could see was a multitude of caves, the green sea of trees, and Stragif's daughters.

A scream echoed from under the canopy. From its direction, a dark shadow rose. Such strength the creature had that it brought parts of the trees with it. The shadow kept going higher and higher, eventually eclipsing the moon itself.

The visage was so terrifying that Morpha let her notebook slip, dropping it far below the trees. Without a second thought, the hatchling dove towards the foliage, and the monstrous shadow soon came after her, like an eagle chasing its prey. Unlike an eagle, though, this creature lacked the finesse of its movements or the regal posture. So, once it collided against the trees, holes in the vegetation were opened far and wide allowing all to see from above the incident underneath them.

Raven could feel it—the despair in Morpha's body. It escaped through her widening eyes and through the scream that followed as the claws of the monster wrapped around her little body. Her notebook was left in tatters, pages floating in the air, soon to touch the ground. Morpha wouldn't touch the ground, however. The dark ave soon began its rising, the little owl trapped inside one of his clasped claws.

Stragif hit the face of the creature at high speed, but it did not even flinch. With a movement of its wings, it sent Stragif flying amongst the branches below.

"Oh, no!" Phorma screamed as she watched her father being struck down once more.

The monster's gaze turned to her, his dark eyes creating a luminescent white reflection of the moon. One would not notice the black color of its irises in such a situation.

Phorma took flight in the opposite direction, trying to get as far away as possible. In the trees underneath her, she saw it, though— the shadow cast by the monster's silhouette growing in size, ever approaching her. Soon, she found herself covered under the darkness brought by such a being. He opened his empty claw to capture her, but suddenly, the light of Murdek shone over Phorma once again. The shadow was lifted by Raven's collision against the monstrous ave.

The shadow now put himself in pursuit of Raven.

Raven took flight, feeling the wind's direction as the tip of his wings touched the winds' paths, searching for one that would lead him in the opposite direction of Phorma's location.

I can't go into the forest. He might hurt the little one, Raven thought to himself, remaining over the trees. *But how will I save her?*

The enormous monster fast approached; he was far more skilled at flying on the Land than Raven was. Raven flapped his wings downwards, and the heavy, cold air moved down, pushing him up. The creature flew straight past him, as it couldn't stop its own momentum.

Raven set his sights on Murdek flying above them. And towards it, he flew. The giant creature changed its course and soon continued the chase.

The higher Raven went, the less air he had around to support him. Now, he could feel it properly—where each current ended, where each path led. None would route him to the moon, but this time, that would be his salvation.

Soon, the void took hold over the Land's atmosphere, and Raven couldn't sustain himself in the air. He gave a final look at the stars and turned around. His descent had begun.

When he turned, he noticed the mysterious ave was also falling down, flapping its wings in despair, attempting to remain in place but failing to do so. Amidst all this movement, the weakness from the lack of air settled in, and his grasp opened, setting Morpha free on her own fall.

But the creature wouldn't let that happen. It turned down towards the Land, opening its beak.

"No! I won't let you hurt her!" Raven screamed—or tried to, at least.

"I'll hurt and kill as much as I want," the bird shouted back.

"No, you won't! Don't you know the Laws, beast? The Creator is the only one that gives life. He is the only one with the authority to take it!"

Silver fire engulfed Raven's feathers, their ends transcending into the color of a rainbow. Raven didn't notice that, however, as he plunged down. This time, he was the hunter.

The wind gained a life of its own, moving as its master demanded, halting the fall of the dark ave.

The two immense birds collided in the air. From the distance, they were a single entity: a ball of flames falling down. Raven passed by Morpha, the winds he commanded stalling her fall enough for him to see Stragif, with broken feathers all around, flying to catch his daughter. They kept falling, ever downwards, until they met the Land. A beam of light escaped from the collision point, and for a second, the day greeted the forest earlier than was nature's course.

When Raven came to his senses, dawn had truly arrived. He wasn't at the crater he recalled creating but, instead, inside a cave, his body covered by foliage neatly attached by bendable branches. Although hydra and food were left for him, no one was around to greet him with a "good morning."

CHAPTER 3

The Mysterious Birds

Hydra dropped constantly, each droplet reverberating on its own demise as it touched the marble rock inside the dark, damp cave.

Zola hated this place. Confined and hidden away from all prying eyes—especially from the eyes of an Owl ready to record their existence in the annals of history—the cave was the perfect hideout for ones such as her family. None would ever dare to enter it.

Still, Zola hated it, no matter the protection it offered.

"***Out of my way!***" screamed a giant dark bird. He wasn't so much flying as he was dragging his body through the mud across the rocky floor of the cave.

"Brother!" Zola exclaimed, running to his side. "What happened to you?"

"What are you doing, girl?" her brother screamed back at her. "Don't you see I'm hurt? Treat me!"

Zola quickly ran around the cave, gathering moss and mushrooms. She mixed them, creating a grim-looking, odorless paste. She approached a small pond created by the nearby hydrafall that ran inside their hideout, stopping by to mix the paste with the flowing hydra.

A chill wind blew from the depths, singing a song as it passed through the rocks. Zola felt called by it; she desperately wanted to know who was signing. She wanted to do so much more, see so much more, and maybe…

"*Zola*! Why are you taking so long!"

But now, all she was doing was preparing a medicinal mixture for her brother. Reality greeted her faster than her dreams or imagination.

"I'm sorry, Zephyr. I was lost in thought."

"That's all you do. You think too much."

"But don't you ever wonder," she began while applying the paste across her brother's wounds, "about us, why we are so different-"

"I told you," he said with rancor, "we are vultures. Don't waste time wondering."

"But that is the name *you* gave us. We don't know what—"

"Argghhhh," the large vulture screamed. "Be mindful where you touch!"

"I'm sorry, I—" The wing of her brother smacked her in her face. She dropped the little urn she used to store the paste. It shattered faster than her dreams of a better life.

"I'm sorry. I'll prepare more," she said, fleeing from his side to get another jar.

"'I'm sorry,' a new voice spoke, trying to imitate her with a satirical tone. "That is all I'm good for: to say how sorry I am."

Another one joined the chorus. "I'm sorry," they kept saying, laughing between one another.

Zola ignored her three brothers just as much as she ignored the dampness of the cave. They were always present, and yet, she wished they were never there.

"What happened to you, bro?" one of the brothers asked the injured vulture.

"There is a weird, dark ave roaming this place," he said with hate in his voice. "The… The… *monster* had the audacity to defy me!"

Another dark ave? Could he be one of us? Of our kind? Zola wondered to herself as she watched her reflection in the pond while filling another urn with hydra. Unlike her three brothers, Zola had deep blue eyes, easy to spot in her beautiful body.

"We need to do something about him," one of the brothers said.

"It might be the ave I've heard so much about, a strange one that spends the whole day not flying but hiding away in a cave," another mentioned.

"We need to show him what vultures are capable of," the third added.

"Don't worry," Zephyr said with a maniacal grin. "We'll take care of him. He won't remain as he is, even if I have to tear his wings apart forever."

Zola shivered at the thought. She had seen far too many atrocities committed by her violent brothers.

"Zola!" Zola heard from a distance. "Do I need to slap you once again to make you move?"

Zola quickly ran to help Zephyr, ignoring every word said by her family. The only thing she listened to was the song of the wind.

In the corner of the room, watching it all unfold, stood a fifth vulture. She observed in silence, watching her sister do all the chores.

"What happened to that one?" Zephyr asked. "Was it your fault, Zaki?"

"Zuri? Nah, she is a smart girl. She knows silence is the best thing those two can do," Zaki replied.

"Zemir," Zephyr began, "you're the smart one, help me to find a way to hunt that strange bird down. We're gonna get rid of him."

The night had fallen once again, but no one would notice from inside the cave. Zola waited for her brothers to go out and about chasing their prey before she herself left.

"Where are you going?" the injured brother asked.

"I'm… going to hunt food for you, as you can't fly for a while," she lied. Zola had other plans for the evening.

"Do you mock me? Do you dare to mock me?"

"No, brother, but I need to do something, don't you think? Something other than saying that I'm sorry."

"*We* hunt," Zephyr said. "You and Zuri do not dare to do our duties. Why can't you be obedient like her?"

Zola took a look at Zuri, going about her duties in the cave in deep silence. *I don't want to live like her, keeping silent to not be mistreated. I want to talk. I want so much more.* "I'll just get some fresh air and see if I can find better medicine for you," Zola said. "Zuri can watch over you."

Her brother didn't respond, and so she took her leave.

All life in the forest moved away from Zola as she silently moved under the trees' crowns. She knew that the Aves and other creatures of the night could see her, for their eyes were created to do so. It was her blue eyes that gave away her presence to the Aves of the day. This slight difference made her different from them in more aspects than just appearance.

Creatures created to hunt in the night, she thought. *What was I created for? Maybe that mysterious new ave is like us. Maybe he'll know who I am…*

Zola followed the river whose source began at the cave she dwelled in, tracing its flow all the way down to the lake. No one was there—at least, no one she was searching for, for on the shore across from her own stood a flock of birds drinking.

Zola quietly made her way around the lake, moving inside the shadows of the forest. *If I approach from behind, they won't see my eyes,* she proudly told herself.

"Excuse me," Zola said, moving out of the shadows.

"Creator's plumage, it's the monster!"

"We're gonna die," exclaimed another ave, pushing his friend towards Zola.

"No, I just want to—" Zola tried to say, but an ave threw a rock at her.

"Fly, everyone! Away from the lake," another one exclaimed.

"I just… wanted to ask you all something," Zola said, but there was no one left to hear it.

With her head hurting, she approached the hydra to take a look at herself. A small cut in her head where the rock had hit her could be seen. Behind her reflection stood a background of dark clouds overcasting the sky. She stared at her face for minutes, with one word repeating in her head over and over again: *monster.*

The sky opened for the rain to fall down, and the visage of her own face became murky, vanishing between the wAves—a disturbance created by the droplets of rain breaking the perfect, calm mirror she'd stared at for so long.

She rose towards the clouds. If the creatures were to see her, so they should. At least for a second, this monster would enjoy her freedom.

And it was there, above the familiar forest, that she saw another bird flying majestically in the rain as if the hydra loved him. He wasn't like her; his feathers were more dark silver than black. But she knew, from that second, that he was unique as, even from that distance, she saw in his eyes—gazing to something beyond the clouds—the same pain she saw when she looked at herself.

The mysterious silver bird took himself into a plunge and dived towards the Land. Zola wanted to know more about him, and so she decided to follow him.

Deep in the forest, she went. Zola stood far away from him, hidden behind the leAves of a tree, immersed in the humidity of the rainfall.

Hydra dropped constantly, each droplet reverberating on its own demise as it touched the foliage of the trees and the Land below, wetting a dark, damp forest. And for the first time in Zola's life, she enjoyed it. She knew she was about to learn something new.

CHAPTER 4

A Road Back Home

The rain kept on falling from the stars, even though the clouds beyond prevented Raven from gazing towards them. That night, he decided not to stand by his usual spot by the lake, aware now that the rain would disturb any reflection. Instead, he rested in another place filled with hydra that would keep him feeling closer to home: the crater created the day he fell—now a small lake where life was thriving.

"Woo. Woo," rushed suddenly from a carved hollow inside a tree. By now, Raven had grown used to his eternal stalker, aided by the fact that he would never approach him.

To his surprise, tonight, of all nights, the owl decided to draw close.

"Good evening, Lord Raven, woo," the ave said, flying out of the tree's trunk. "I hope I'm not bothering you on this… joyful evening. My name is Stragif, Stragif Strigiformes," he finished while wiping his glasses off from countless droplets of hydra.

"You don't need to call me 'Lord.' I hope you're doing fine this evening as well," Raven replied, hydra falling in his eyes. "Nice to officially meet you. Are the little ones alright?"

"Indeed, they are, woo," Stragif replied. "A bit too scared to leave the nest for a while, but they'll come around." Stragif returned his glasses to where they belonged, on top of his beak, but soon, he couldn't see Raven once again.

"I appreciate the food and hydra you left for me," Raven began, "I assume they came from you."

"They came, woo, from my daughter. It was her idea."

"And what of the ave that pursued us? I hope you'll forgive me, but I can't recall what happened with it," Raven asked, moving around the place, trying to find a good spot to have a talk without interruption from the hydra's bullseye ability to obscure his vision.

"He ran away, woo," Stragif replied, taking his glasses off once again while following Raven's movement, "quite literally. You did such damage to him that he could barely flap his wings."

"I hope I didn't hurt him too much," Raven replied with a thoughtful tone. "It would be imprudent of me to shout the Fourth Law and proceed to deliver a fatal blow on an ave. Someone would be really sad with me if I did anything else wrong."

"Who is that someone you speak of, Lord— I'm sorry… Raven?" Stragif questioned him, moving under a group of branches.

"It doesn't matter," Raven replied in sadness. "At this point, I don't think we will ever be together again." As he finished his words, Raven briefly looked towards the sky and saw nothing but hydra falling down.

"Lord… Oh, I apologize, woo. It's a bad habit of mine," Stragif said. "Raven, I came here to repay you for saving my family. Is there anything I might be able to help you with?"

"If I can't help myself, surely there would be not a single ave on the Land that would be capable of achieving such a feat," Raven said in sorrow.

"Try me, woo. I'm an Owl. There are very few things my kind might not know."

After a few seconds of hesitation, Raven finally decided to open up. "I need to go home." He almost shed a tear by putting out these words, but Stragif would never notice it—the rain would wash it away.

"And where is home? You share no resemblance with anything I have ever seen or read about, so I can't pinpoint a location on my own," Stragif quickly replied, his tone filled with curiosity.

"You see, my friend, there are things you don't know in the end."

"Don't be pessimistic, woo. I've seen many maps before. Tell me a place, and I can point you in the direction you need to go. No one needs to know everything, just enough."

Raven let a sigh escape before giving a more precise answer. "I'm from a place called Murdek. Have you ever heard of it?"

"Murdek, woo?" Stragif's head bobbed from one side to another. "The name sounds familiar, but I can't seem to recall it. Where exactly is it?"

"On the moon," Raven let out. Stragif's eyes widened with such a response.

"How can something be on the moon, woo? I'm speechless."

"Just as Delmartica is on the sun, Murdek is on the moon. I was born there, by the side of my partner Starlight. She was to teach me the ways of living—the secrets of creation and the Creator. But one day, she forbade me from doing something, and in my hubris, I decided to do it regardless, following my curiosity. I approached a star, and the price I paid was to fall from the moon all the way down to the Land." Raven told this story in a somber tone, almost as a reflection to himself.

"Forget calling you 'Lord,' woo. I should be calling you a god!"

"No, please, I don't deserve such a title. I've failed in my duties, and I shall be addressed as Raven for doing so."

"Raven, there might be a solution to your problem, woo. But I can't say for sure."

"Tell me," Raven cried in despair. "Tell what to do, I beg of you!"

Taken aback, Stragif began, sharing a tale of old. "During the creation of the Five Laws, woo, back in the Dark Years of Madness, it's said that the goddess, Sunshine, and the goddess, Starlight, descended from the place they live to communicate with us. The place to which they descended is called Mount Kingdom Come. Any who seek to commune with the goddesses themselves should travel to said place."

"And where is this mountain located?" Raven eagerly asked.

"No one knows, woo. The myth says that the Land will show the way for those who need it," Stragif replied in disappointment.

"I don't know anything about the Land. Could you come with me? You believe in me, don't you?" Raven's desperation increased. There was a semblance of hope blooming in his chest.

"I do believe in you, Raven, woo. You fell from the sky with a rainbow. You plunged a bird down from the atmosphere. You're unique. But I have a family. I can't just leave them."

The blooming hope suddenly spoiled itself; its petals were ground into dust.

"I'll see if I can get some concrete info, woo. Hopefully, I can point you in the right direction," Stragif said, preparing to fly away.

Raven wanted to say something, but he didn't know what. He stood there, with the rain pouring through the space between the branches, washing away his dreams of ever returning.

I need to learn more about this place… And I need a guide.

"What? I can't believe you just left him there!" Stragif's wife screamed back at him.

"What did you expect me to do, woo?"

"At least, bring him here. He is a god! One that saved our daughter!"

"But Griphi, what did you expect me to do? If a god doesn't know how to help himself, how could I do so?"

"By being on his side during this journey," she replied, using a maternal tone. "Don't you see he is nothing but a child? He is no different from our daughters, disobeying his elder and paying a price for it."

"I understand, woo," Stragif replied with a deep sigh, "but with that strange bird still lurking around, I can't leave my family in such a dangerous place."

"A god fell from the sky, a strange bird lurks around a place it clearly doesn't belong… Can't you see? There is something happening. Our daughters' future might be tied to this."

"I can see, but… I just don't know what to do."

Stragif approached a bookshelf containing all the knowledge collected by him and his family across generations of recording the long nights of yore. His eyes searched for a book that could help, but he found none. If he had a clue as to the whereabouts of Mount Kingdom Come, he certainly would've used it to give his family a better position in the Order.

With a glance, sitting over the table, he noticed torn pages lying across a dirty notebook. They were Morpha's. Written on one of the pages, he saw the words "Stragif, the Rainbow Hunter"—words that put a smile on his face…

…and a thought in his head.

He turned towards his two daughters, sleeping next to one another, still recovering from the terrible events from last night. "Griphi, you're right. I'll help him and do my diligent duty as an Owl," Stragif said in melancholy. "Our daughters will have a future. Our family will be remembered."

And with that, Stragif collected an empty book from his bookshelf. To the first page, he attached Morpha's torn writing, envisioning it to be a title page. Next, he collected a map of the Land and folded it inside the notebook.

Not too long after, he approached both girls, waking them up and telling them of the journey he was about to undertake. Though he'd expected a confrontation, the two girls responded in kindness with doubts reserved to themselves.

"It's our fault, isn't it?" Phorma asked.

"No, my dear, it's the will of the Creator that put Raven on our doorstep, woo," Stragif said.

"I'm scared, you know?" Morpha began, hiding away tears that clearly wanted to be seen. "But I think you have to do it. I truly think…" She looked away briefly towards Griphi, allowing a single tear to fall.

The four Aves joined together, sharing a powerful embrace. The cold brought by feathers drowning in rain was suppressed under the warmth of good feelings.

"It's time for the tale of Stragif, the Rainbow Hunter, to begin, woo," Stragif said with confidence.

That brought not a tear to Morpha's eyes but a smile to her face.

Stragif flew all the way back to where Raven stood. Protecting the book he carried with him was a piece of fabric from Phorma's scarf. In the darkness of the night, the red shone bright.

As he approached the place where he'd last seen Raven, Stragif couldn't help but feel watched. Something with piercing blue eyes hid itself from the prying eyes of others, being too far away for Stragif to find some familiarity in their complexion. And as far as he was concerned, this time, he was not there to document and learn in the night nor to hunt or survive. He was around to help a friend in need. And at the same place he left Raven alone, there stood the giant silver ave.

"Good evening, once again, woo," Stragif said, flying down towards a branch under a spot where the hydra precipitation would have difficulty finding him.

"You returned!" Raven exclaimed. "Tell me you've found something."

"I found nothing useful, I'm afraid, woo, but I bear good tidings. I shall join you in your adventure. We shall find the way together."

"And how can we find the way if we don't know where to start?" Raven asked impatiently.

It was at that moment that the rain ceased to be. Shining over the mountains, the light of Murdek passed through the clouds, piercing a place that seemed to be far, far away beyond those insurmountable slabs of stone covered in ice.

"We shall follow the Land's guidance," Stragif answered with a confidence he had never felt. "Woo."

CHAPTER 5

A Difficult Journey

Dawn had yet to greet the Land by the time Raven and Stragif reached the actual mountain range, soaring far above the ground. The arid and inhospitable place was quite stunning under Raven's eyes as, for the first time, he could see a different color other than the green sea he'd grown so used to. Whatever was beyond the range kept itself invisible to the eye, for as far as the eye could see, there were only mountains, more mountains, and to the surprise of the two, more mountains.

A faraway group composed of three enormous triangle-shaped rocks was impressive, overshadowing anything and everything. In the surrounding area, the peaks had had snow for days. Thankfully, though, the section just after the forest was no more than rock over sand, far too low to have any snow on it.

"Dawn will break soon, woo," Stragif said, concerned. "We need to find a spot to rest."

But as much as they tried, no place that could offer shade for the day could be seen.

"What about caves?" Raven questioned. "The forest had so many, I recall going to the wrong one multiple times."

"We should find some around, woo. My maps told me about a river nearby that flows from one."

But as far as the eye could see, there was no river around. Flying along the valleys, Raven spotted a trail similar to a road but not made by any terrestrial animal. Instead, it shaped itself very similar to a natural formation, ebbing and flowing between the ranges.

"What is that?" Raven asked, pointing at the strange road.

The first rays of sunlight suddenly broke through the darkness behind Raven. He felt it, even without it touching him, the looming gloom of fire burning his feathers.

"Seems like an old riverbed, woo," Stragif replied, fatigue rising.

"Is there a cave nearby?" Raven asked, his throat feeling dry by now.

"Like in the forest, woo? Maybe?" Stragif said, his eyes weighing on him, closing slowly.

"Let's go down there," Raven suggested, "follow the dry section as if the river was still there—" But before he could finish, Stragif collapsed from the sky.

Raven quickly put himself into a downward plunge, increasing his speed as much as he could to reach Stragif's falling body. He felt at ease doing so, feeling a hint of the winds obeying him for a second—but just a second. When he was just about to touch Stragif, fire enveloped his body, and the wind dispersed.

Raven continued his plunge, grabbing Stragif with his claws, careful to not burn his newfound friend, and quickly changing direction, flying towards the shadow created by the top of a peak. A piece of paper flew from inside Stragif's little bag, catching fire as soon as it approached Raven's body.

With the fire burning even brighter in front of his eyes as the sun climbed ever higher in the sky, Raven lost control of himself, not noticing that right in front of him stood a giant piece of rock.

"That was the map, woo," Stragif muttered in utter despair, "made by some of the greatest Owls of the past."

"I'm sorry," Raven replied, spending his time under a set of rocks built like a little tent. Stragif seemed to know how to do many things.

"You have nothing to apologize for, woo. That is the second time you have saved my life. And that was the second night in a row my life was in danger."

"No wonder you can't sleep properly," Raven responded, feeling thirsty. "Do you know where we are?"

"No, woo, but I can hazard a guess using the large mountains and the dry riverbed we found earlier."

The mention of hydra made Raven even thirstier and caused him to notice a second thing: He had not eaten for a long while now. "I'm sorry to ask, but I'm feeling thirsty. Do you know where we might be able to find hydra here?"

"I recall seeing a village located nearby, woo. We might find hydra there."

"How do we get there?"

"I don't know, woo. The map I had is kind of burned right now. I expected we would reach it or see it by now."

"Should we return to the forest, then? Equip ourselves better for the trip?" *Maybe the clouds parting wasn't a sign. Perhaps it was just a coincidence,* Raven told himself, his mind not really capable of thinking clearly about anything other than food and hydra.

Stragif stared at the soil, contemplating the rocks, clearly lost in deep thought.

"Stay here, woo. I'll search for food and hydra," Stragif said. There was a small hint of sadness in his tone. "I won't disappoint you, Raven. I promise," he finished, taking flight.

"Are you sure you're alright? You seem sleepy and—" By then, Stragif had vanished from sight behind the rocky cliff.

You and I are so alike, Raven thought. *We are both creatures of the night. How can such a bright and warm thing hinder us so much?*

As Raven muttered those thoughts to himself, he tried to approach the sunlight, desperate to feel its warmth.

In an instant, Raven's mind traveled back in time: He saw a version of himself gliding next to a star, almost touching it. Then, all of a sudden, he was back in the frigid and arid mountains, seeing nothing but the jagged rocks that surrounded him.

The more I learn, the less I understand. Should I not strive to understand things? he thought, looking at his rocky roof.

The sound of rocks moving on their own reached Raven's ears. For a time, there was silence, soon broken by more rocky slides. Unlike the forest, the sounds of the mountains were completely unfamiliar to Raven.

"Stragif?" he asked in a low voice. He received no answer. "Stragif?" he asked louder. In answer, the rocks moved once again, some fell right in front of his tent. Whatever was causing it was now quite close to him.

Something heavy suddenly landed on top of Raven's tent. The dust from the rock fell in his eyes. *That was far too loud to be Stragif,* he thought, eyes closing and burning with tears trying to purify them from the invasive dust.

With eyes semi-open, Raven saw a silhouette moving in the front of the tent. The complexion belonged to an ave he had never seen before—one far larger and more imposing than Stragif.

"To think you'd trouble yourself to fly all the way up here, friend," the ave spoke. "And to think you'd hide in such a strange contraption. You're clearly as strange as they say."

"Who are you?" Raven asked, his heart pounding faster and his body shivering. Since the day of the fall, he had not felt such strength of emotion.

The ave cried to the sky, and one by one, Raven heard the sound of different birds landing around his tent.

"Monster from the Kingdom of the Owls, the mountains will not allow you to rage terror in here," the ave spoke as if declaring something. "You won't reach our village."

"No!" Raven shouted. "This is a misunderstanding. The ave you seek is still in the forest."

"Remove the rocks," the ave ordered.

"*No!*" Raven screamed. "If you do that, bad things might happen to us all."

"The only bad thing in this place is you," the ave replied.

Before Raven had the chance to say another word, dust fell once again into his eyes—this time, by the force of beings pushing the rock upwards.

The warmth touched Raven's skin in a span of seconds, sending him back to the agonizing pain he'd rather have forgotten while blinding the Aves around him with resplendent light.

Stragif was following the dry river bed, hoping a settlement had been formed near its margins. It didn't take him much time to find a series of nests laid atop a multitude of peaks and by the wayside of an enormous cliff dropping into a valley far below.

What is going on here? he wondered as he saw mountain eagles lying weak all around. Their eyes were devoid of any strength that they might have once had.

"Excuse me," Stragif said, approaching one of the nests. "Me and my friend are in search of hydra and food for a trip. Is there any place I can find supplies?"

Stragif's eyes threatened to close once again.

"Aren't you too far away from your Kingdom, little owl?" replied the eagle. "You must be desperate, walking around when you should be asleep." The final words were spoken with great difficulty.

"I'm just passing by the region with my friend, woo. Please, could you provide us with some help?"

At the center of the village, Stragif noticed caskets filled with hydra near a great peak shaped like a needle, filled with nests. Most of the caskets were dry, and those that had any hydra left were at least half-empty.

"I can't, and I'm afraid no one around here can," the mountain eagle said. "The river has been dry for weeks. The storm in your Kingdom has scared our prayers, and the forest at the edge of the range possesses no life for us to pray upon."

"But what of those caskets I see, woo? The ones next to the strange structure."

"They are for the guards and hunters of the mountain," the ave replied. "Of late, we've been hearing rumors of a strange dark ave, enormous in size, hunting prey in your area."

Another mountain eagle approached them. Albeit far larger than Stragif, the ave was skinny, the feathers on its body designed with the lack of anything to cover but skin and bones.

"Strange owl, please return to your Kingdom or find a different passage," the new mountain eagle said. "There is nothing here but death, of late."

The two mountain eagles looked at each other for a brief moment before the newcomer continued with his speech. The mountain eagle took flight and began to circle around the small town, preparing to shout an announcement. "All residents, please proceed to the emergency shelter with your eggs," he announced. "We have detected at least four strange, dark Aves flying around our city borders. Our guards are currently engaging one of those Aves."

Four, woo? How can it be…

The mountain eagle that Stragif had previously engaged with stood up from her idle position, revealing a couple of eggs underneath her.

"Dear owl," she began, "would you help me bring my babies inside the cave by the cliff? I feel like I wouldn't be able to carry a single one by myself, let alone two."

A cave, woo? That could be useful.

"Of course, woo. I shall help you."

Stragif took the book out of his purse and replaced it with both eggs. He quickly felt the weight increasing as each egg was left under his care, but the cloth was strong enough to keep them safe. Stragif followed the mountain eagles, flying inside a cave hidden by the cliff.

Sad eyes watched as the owl entered the dry cave. If they wanted to demonstrate any shock regarding this occurrence, they couldn't. All their energy had been sapped by the conditions they were living under.

"What happened here, woo?" Stragif asked, entering and moving across the cave with caution to not break an egg, searching for a spot to land.

"A rainbow fell from the sky," the mother of the eggs replied, "and soon, all water ceased to be, every storm moved towards the forests, and the river dried."

"Really, woo? Surely, you don't believe the rainbow to be the cause of it all," Stragif said, noticing that the cave had been adorned with different statues and paintings depicting the Creator and the Mountain Eagles. Each stroke showed how they lived their lives: in fight, in hunt, and in protection of the mountain.

"We don't know," she replied, helping Stragif to set the eggs in a comfy place. "All we know is that such a beautiful thing had to be a sign from the Creator. A test, maybe?" she said with peaceful eyes watching over her little eggs.

"He is on fire!" someone shouts in the distance. "Stay away from him!"

Oh no, Raven!

Without hesitation, Stragif set out to rescue his friend.

The cold air was no more, as silver flames burned the surroundings, heating it up.

"Formation!" shouted one of the guards. All the eagles took flight, surrounding Raven, flying a circle around him.

There was something different in the air, and it wasn't heat. It was a call, a vibration telling Raven something, pointing deep down inside the earth. Something hidden. Whatever this was did not simply speak with him but communicated with a primordial instinct all beings possessed: thirst.

Compelled by it, Raven soared closer to the soil, the eagles following him from above.

The eagle furthest from him assumed a hunting position in the air, aiming at Raven and launching himself at him. In the blink of an eye, the ave landed its powerful claws on Raven's skin.

The two screamed—Raven for the damage it caused him; the eagle for the fire that burned its claws and quickly spread to its feathers.

"Stay away from me. I don't want to hurt anyone," Raven screamed, trying to open his eyes, but the flames and the dust that settled in prevented it.

"Over here, woo!" Raven heard the shout coming from somewhere distant. He didn't need to think, he knew who it belonged to and what to do next.

"Stragif! I can't see! Guide me, please," he screamed back, waiting for his friend to reply. In truth, his instincts were still calling for him to dive inside the Land itself, something he knew would accomplish nothing.

"Follow my voice, woo. There is a cave nearby."

Raven changed his trajectory, following Stragif's command. The strange feeling intensified. In the darkness, he saw rivers flowing under the land, calling to him. But the rivers led him astray, and he chose to believe in his friend.

"He is flying towards the village!" one of the guards shouted. "Attack him at all costs!"

The eagles changed formation, creating a line in the sky, ready to dive toward the creature they meant to hunt. One after the other, they did so, flying like arrows released by a cannon, not a bow, reaching Raven in a mere instant.

None of them had a pleasant experience.

"I told you all," Raven screamed, "I don't want to hurt anyone! Just stay away."

He reached the village soon after burning most of the Eagle Guard. Flying without direction, he stumbled over the caskets of hydra, the fire vaporizing it in an instant.

"Our water! This monster destroyed our water!" exclaimed one of the eagles.

"He will kill us all!" cried another guard in despair.

"To me, my friends," called the eagle flying above the village—the one Stragif had just spoken to. "Let's end this, once and for all."

All of a sudden, an eagle jumped at Stragif, bringing him down with ease.

"You won't guide him to bring our demise, owl," the Eagle guard said.

"No, woo! You don't understand. He is just in pain!" Stragif replied, his face on the ground.

"Stragif, where are you?" Raven shouted, but he couldn't see.

Stragif tried to open his beak, but the eagle strengthened the clasp of his claws on him and pushed his face down toward the dirty, arid soil. He couldn't say a word.

"Stragif?" Raven screamed in despair, his body hitting all he could see, feel, and touch.

The eagles assumed a circle formation above the village.

"Stragif, please. I need you!"

The eagles locked eyes with Raven's position.

"Let's end this, my cherished companions, even if it burns us to death!" Lord Thebas of the guard ordered.

"***Stragif, please!***" Raven screamed, his flames changing color, the dark silver hue transcending all the colors of the rainbow.

"What, in all creation, is this?" Lord Thebas shouted, the light blinding his view.

The wind picked up around Raven. He was tired, he was burned, he was afraid, and he was thirsty—very thirsty. He felt the vibration calling from the ground and directed the wind towards it. The flames followed it, and so fierce they were that the soil began to melt away. No sooner than that, water flew from the ground, the turbulent stream flooding the bottom section of the town.

The eagle holding Stragif took flight, pulling Stragif with him. So shocked was the ave that he couldn't keep the clasp around Stragif tight enough to prevent the owl from escaping, and that was what Stragif did. The eagle did not care as the color reflected all of the rainbow, becoming a majestic new sun burning at the center of their little, forsaken town.

"Woo. Woo," Stragif called with all the strength he had left.

And when Raven heard it—the sound of a friend who had been looking out for him—he felt strangely at home.

The flames died back down to their original silver colors. "Woo. Woo," guided him. Soon enough, Raven's flames dissipated, for he was inside a cave.

A small crack showed up on the surface of one of the little eggs, with a tiny beak trying to break through. The second egg shook and rolled around, and after a while, a crack appeared on it, too.

"We need to help them!" Raven exclaimed. "They can't break free."

"There is no need, woo," Stragif replied. "This is their first test of life."

"This is so hard to look at," Raven complained.

"Don't worry too much," said the eagle mother. "You also had to go through the same trouble, great Raven."

But try as he might to reassure himself, Raven couldn't remember the moment he left his egg. Seconds later, one of the eggs fully broke, and a little hatchling eagle came out of it. Less than seconds later, another one popped out.

Lord Thebas and Queen Aquilla approached both of them. "Welcome to the Land, little ones," Lord Thebas said.

The family embraced in tenderness—a scene that touched Stragif deeply. Raven observed the moment, watching the interlocked eyes of the parents hearing the cries of the little hatchlings.

"Everything is ready," a third eagle said, gesturing behind them. "I hope the two days of rest afforded you the nourishment you both needed," he said, giving canteens with hydra to the traveling companions.

"Are you sure you don't want to rest a while more? We owe you that much," Lord Thebas said.

"We must travel east, beyond the range," Raven said. "Mount Kingdom Come surely will be there."

"There is nothing but a desert that way," Lord Thebas replied, "a dead land with nothing around. I'm afraid your mountain is just a myth."

"Yes," the mother interjected. "You see, here, my little hatchlings are the true Mount Kingdom. Come—my connection with the Creator who gave them life."

"I appreciate the help," Raven said, preparing to take flight. Next to statues depicting Sunshine and Starlight, the cave now had paintings of a bird surrounded by a rainbow, bringing water to a dead village. "But my journey is far from over, and I know, deep in my heart, I'll find the way."

"Your miracle won't be forgotten," the mother said. "My children and their children will tell of this day. They shall know that the Creator sent us an ave to save us all."

The two friends took flight, leaving the cave behind in the middle of the night.

Soon, hours had passed, and speckles of ice adorned Raven's feathers little by little, turning his silver visage into pure white. Flying over the tallest snow peak, the air grew thinner by the minute while the winds picked up a downward stream, making flight incredibly complicated.

Soon after, the mountain itself vanished from view, for a snowstorm grew in intensity, transforming into a whiteout. Eventually, they gave up for the night, landing with great difficulty on the west side of a cliff, for when the sun rose from the east, the peak would protect Raven from its burning light.

After finding a safe spot, Stragif burned some of the pages from his notebook, kindling a fire that he thought came from the effort of his family to protect and support him, even from afar.

"Stragif, why did the captain of the Mountain Guard and his wife look at each other so tenderly?" Raven asked.

"That is because they love one another, woo. They can see each other's soul that way."

"Love? I've heard this word many times from Starlight about the love the Creator has for all creation. Was it love that gave life to the little ones?" Raven asked, watching the flames moving left and right, fighting against the cold wind to stay alive.

"Indeed, it was. Love can build many things," Stragif said. "Just like this flame, it burns deep into one's soul and fights against adversity to bring life into this world or to bring culture and order, such as our love for the Creator. Me and my partner, we both love one another deeply, which makes this trip harder as I miss her so much."

Partner, huh? I am Starlight's partner, and I miss her and all of Murdek so much, Raven told himself.

The next night, the two set off from the largest peak, following their way eastward, eventually reaching the end of the range.

"You two surely are weird," came a voice echoing across the deep valleys below them. Raven and Stragif stopped mid-flight, trying to find the place from which the voice originated.

"That trick you pulled with the eagles was quite interesting," a new voice added, his location just as hidden as the first.

"Tell me," the first voice said. "What did you do to my sister? Did you burn her like you did to those poor guards?"

"Sister? What sister?" Raven shouted back.

"I recognize this voice, woo," Stragif said, his mind flashing back to a dark, damp cave and his terrified daughters under his wings.

"Liar," the second voice proclaimed. "I bet you killed her!"

"I never killed anyone," Raven retorted. "Those guards were burned, but they live. They do—"

Two enormous shadows lifted themselves from under the snow, surrounding Raven and Stragif.

"Liar," the Stranger called, staring deeply into Raven's eyes. "'Only the Creator can give life, and only the Creator can take it.' You spoke those words, and yet, you took my sister away from me." For someone looking deep inside Raven's soul, he certainly didn't shed a single drop of that "love" feeling Stragif spoke about the previous night. "I hope you forgive me if I want some revenge. That is the second time you've done something against me, after all."

The winds picked up once again, a heavy current pushing everything down, bringing with it snow from the clouds above.

"Hold on to me, Stragif," Raven shouted, noticing the two large birds ready to attack them. Stragif did as he said and landed right on top of Raven.

Raven looked toward the end of the range, where a giant sand cloud was traversing the border between desert and mountain range. The wind changed direction, moving then to the east, towards the desert.

The Land talks to me, Raven reveled inside his mind. Raven flew upwards towards the atmosphere once again.

"I won't be tricked twice, little bird," the Stranger called from down below, following Raven's trajectory without giving proper chase.

Snow began to pile down in ever greater quantities. Soon, the entire range was under a monochromatic shroud. Raven allowed his lift to vanish and glided downward, letting the eastward wind carry him.

"Do you know where we are going, woo?" Stragif shouted, the cold snow and heavy winds muffling his voice.

Raven kept his eyes wide open, noticing dark shadows moving left and right, trying to find him. *Strange. My eyes might be deceiving me, but I think I can see three dark shadows moving about.*

Suddenly, the air grew thicker, and the cold began to erode. The gentle snow grew grizzled, mixing with arid sand.

The whiteout was now black, and Raven could not keep his eyes open any longer, the sand becoming far more dense than the snow. He just kept flying, his wings getting heavier by the second as sand piled on them far faster than snow did.

"Don't follow him," the Stranger shouted. His voice had a dark, grim tone as if he had won.

"But if they escape, we won't know what happened to Zola," the other voice replied.

"Forget Zola. We'll have our revenge—"

The duo was then too far, and too deep into the sandstorm to hear the mysterious bird's voice as he continued, "Zuri and Zemir should've found the owl's nest by now. If they survive this trip, we'll have a nice little gift for them."

The world was scorching. The Land burned alive as the sands of the desert moved like a thunderous sea. Raven burned with it.

The sandstorm carried them far into the heart of the desert. So distant they were from the mountains that they could no longer see even a hint of the range on the horizon. Sky and sand were all that there was in any direction. And Raven was burning in it.

He couldn't move, he couldn't hide, and he had no energy to fly. Stragif would, from time to time, use hot air currents to easily reach high skies in search of hydra, food, or a place to stay. But nothing was in sight.

On the second day, he thought he'd seen an oasis waiting for them, but it was a mirage. On the third, he'd imagined a cave. On the fourth, he thought he saw a mysterious bird following him, hiding behind the dunes as much as it could. It was a mirage, of course.

The nights were far worse, as the desert was just as gelid as the mountains were, freezing Raven's injuries to a gruesome level. From the injuries sustained by the sunlight, Raven could not properly fly, resorting to moving around in the treacherous, ever-changing sand dunes.

The two traveling companions soon ceased to speak to one another, saving their energy the best they could. They knew, after all, that if they tired themselves too much and found themselves in need of hydra, none would be present around here. Whatever Raven did back in the Mountain Eagles' village, he clearly had no control over it for, as thirsty as he became here, no hydra would call for him to alleviate his pain.

On the fifth day, a sandstorm engulfed them during the day, affording Raven a little bit of respite as the sunlight had some difficulty passing through the dense grains of sand. Unfortunately, it also filled their canteen with sand and made them even more thirsty.

On that same night, both friends found themselves too tired to travel. Stragif sat down, staring at Morpha's drawing in his notebook. In the drawing, he was dressed as a knight, similar to the armory used by the Roosters in their legends and stories but changed to fit an owl and its large head. Surrounding him was a colorful rainbow shining under the stars, one of which caught his attention as it was painted in red rather than the usual white or yellow. His gaze turned up to the sky, and there it was, a red star, shining bright to the east.

"Raven, woo," Stragif said, his voice tired and yet filled with hope. "Get ready for a little walk. I might've found our way out of here."

CHAPTER 6

Kingdom of the Sparrows

The desert winds brought with them three strange fruits that, when cut open, were filled with hydra inside.

"Look, Raven," Stragif said, the usual "woo" clearly missing from his tired voice. "The Creator knows we are on the right path."

Raven did not respond. Even though it was nighttime, he still couldn't afford to fly over the desert; his strength had been burned out by the daylight.

"Here, my friend," Stragif said after drinking from the fruit while tipping one next to Raven's beak. "Drink it."

This tastes horrible, Raven thought, but at the same time, it tasted like perfection.

"It isn't good, is it?" Stragif asked. "I read about those fruits once. They grow from cacti in the desert near the Kingdom of the Sparrows. They provide hydration and nourishment."

A Kingdom? Near such a horrible place? What kind of madness is that? Raven thought.

"This Kingdom, you know, is unique in all the Land," Stragif began, telling a story like a father to his child, this time, trying to keep both awake, for the day took far too much from them. "The lush green and vivid plains that are situated there are trapped all around by the desert, a large range of mountains, and the ocean. Many myths are from there. Maybe the Land is guiding us to hear them."

Every night, Murdek would be visible from afar. That night, though, Raven couldn't find in him the strength to look up and stare at it. His neck was far too burned.

Why, Starlight? Why don't you come down and take me away from here—from this sordid dead world?

Of course, despite his thoughts of desperation, Starlight never replied or dared to show up.

The next day, three more fruits were caught by the winds, and in the night, the two resumed their long walk across the desert; their feet were having trouble walking such a large distance. The night was cold and frigid as always, making it easier to move compared to the burning sands of the day, but the journey was still nothing short of treacherous.

The next day, three fruits were carried by the dunes towards them, but the two didn't need them anymore for, now, cacti were blocking their gaze in every direction they looked. So were the mountains, not as tall as the range they crossed but imposing, nonetheless. Next to the peaks, they could see the lush green lands where the Sparrows lived their whole lives.

"Thank you, great star, for guiding us," Stragif said. "Woo."

That night, they were out of the desert and setting foot in grassy lands. Stragif took the remainder of the silver moonlight to build a small blanket made of grass, tree branches, and leAves. He covered Raven with it, setting his friend aside under some trees in the hope that the daylight wouldn't touch him.

When morning came, and the sun had difficulty touching Raven, the two friends could finally sleep well.

Two days later, Stragif and Raven moved towards the peaks around the Kingdom, where they managed to find a cave for Raven to rest. Moving there was a tricky trek, as Raven still retained all of his bruises and burns. And the cave itself wasn't anywhere near as big as the ones in the Kingdom of the Owls. It would be more accurate to call it a sideways hole rather than a cave proper. Still, it would suffice for the moment.

"What are you doing?" Raven asked Stragif. The bird was covered in tree leAves painted with mud, giving them a brownish color. They were joined together just like Raven's blanket was, forming a cape around the owl.

"Me, woo? I'm going to pay a visit to the Sparrows. Your wounds are too deep. We need proper food and medicine."

"I ask… about your unique… accessories," Raven questioned amidst a crisis of coughs.

"Oh, this, woo?" Stragif replied, moving around in his cape. "The Sparrows are very secretive Aves. They only talk amongst themselves and offer aid seldom. Owls don't travel during the day, so they need to see me as a creature of the day: a sparrow!"

Raven started this conversation confused and that hadn't changed a bit.

"All this secrecy, woo, is what gives them so many myths and legends. 'Keepers of secret treasures,' some would call them. Being in such a unique place, many trades converge here, and still, the Sparrows ignore all bypassers and bystanders. Don't fret, my dear friend, I'll trick them, as us Owls are the most intelligent Aves on the Land, and I shall find you help," Stragif prepared to set off.

"Thank you," Raven said. "The Creator surely gave me the best of friends. I shall never forget this trial I've been putting you through."

"For the one that saved my daughters, woo, there is nothing I wouldn't do."

Far away from the cave, in the middle of a forest where trees were taller than in the Kingdom of the Owls but far more spaced out, stood the capital of the Kingdom of the Sparrows. Seeing it with his own eyes, Stragif felt as if every book he had ever read had lied to him about the beauty of such a place; the prosperous Kingdom was far more beautiful than any word could ever convey.

Set atop the connection between two rivers, the city seemed to float up in the air, businesses built inside the large red and brown tree trunks. Outside them, hanging at the top of the largest tree branches, were their nests. Their yellow hue came from small, dry branches and grass, creating a contrast to the lush green beneath them. Perfect polished poles connected each tree and establishment, creating a means for walking or for rest. And on a small island, at the center of the river junction, a plaza was paved with yellow rocks, laid for all to sit and enjoy the day.

Stragif just couldn't believe it—how tall each tree grew, how large the riverbed was, making the lake next to his home seem like a pond in comparison.

No words could describe such beauty, but every word in the tomes of old perfectly described the Sparrow's temperament, as they were just as hard to talk to and as scary to look at, as expected, frowning all the time as if life had left them with incessant anger.

"Excuse me, woo—" Stragif started to ask someone, but before he could finish or remember to hide his customary greeting, the sparrow flew away. Their brown wings and white body feathers were all that he could make from the ave's fast movement.

"Could you please help me?" Stragif asked inside what seemed to be a medicinal shop. "My friend and I are in dire need of medicine as he is burned and weak."

The store owner looked at him from top to bottom before giving him an apt reply. "How are the burns on your friend's body? Owl-sized?" he asked with a smirk, a piece of grass coming from his mouth as if it was a fashion accessory. Despite that, he had, like any other sparrow, a regal composure unmatched by the greatest of eagles—and now, Stragif had met some to compare against.

Stragif's heart stopped. *Obviously an undocumented saying from the region. He doesn't know who I truly am,* Stragif reassured himself. *I shall document this later.*

"Well, he is… twice, or at least, three times my size… and his whole body is burned pretty much everywhere."

"What did this fellow do? Try to touch the sun hoping to find the Creator earlier?" the shop owner said.

Does he know, woo? Stragif thought in despair. *No, no, he's surely just jesting… Surely.*

"I'm sorry, I should not talk bad about others' suffering, right, fellow sparrow?" the owner continued, crunching the grass in his mouth while looking under the counter for some ointment.

"Here it is," the shop owner said, shoving a small ointment case over the counter. "This should cost you three Lise. You might need about 900 Lise to get enough to cover an ave the size you describe."

"900 what?" Stragif asked in confusion.

"Lise, our currency, fellow sparrow… Even the Owls have it described in their books. Surely, someone that lives here would know of it."

"That— That is not it, w—" But Stragif stopped himself before the whole "woo" could come out. "I'm just surprised by the price. How can I get such an amount of money?"

"A month's work in the King's guard should earn you that much," the shop owner replied, "Any sparrow can get in there, especially one with such a great and strong complexion, unlike any other."

"A month, woo! I don't have that kind of time!"

"Well, then, you won't have the ointment," the shop owner replied, ignoring the woo that escaped.

This might be my chance, Stragif told himself, preparing to ask another question. "My friend will surely die without it," Stragif began, his tone more melodramatic than a theater scene. "Maybe he'll need a miracle. Maybe he would need to reach Mount Kingdom Come…"

"You're wasting your time," the shop owner replied, spitting the grass from his mouth to the floor. The attitude somehow made him even more regal than before. "You can only reach Mount Kingdom Come in death. In a sense, your friend is almost there."

Those words shocked Stragif. *Did the Land guide us toward Raven's death? No! Of course not! The Land is not the Creator, it can't take an ave's life.*

Stragif left the store empty-handed but with his mind filled with dread. So, he walked around asking questions to all that could hear him. Many didn't want to listen, closing their doors in his face or flying to their nests as soon as they saw his approach.

"The Land shall guide you to Mount Kingdom Come," one sparrow said before taking flight.

"We can't help you with your problems," another proclaimed.

A small traveling caravan passed by, not composed of sparrows but of a multitude of different Aves. Stragif approached them in the hopes of gaining some information, food, anything.

"I'm sorry," the caravan leader said. He was a great roadrunner of gray feathers, distinguishable from all the rest. "Me and my friends are here to trade from across the hills and the desert. We can't afford to give away our possessions."

"So, you travel a lot? Have you heard anything about Mount Kingdom Come?"

"What is there to know about it other than what is already told? I've heard many tales about it, from the Land showing you the way to it being in your heart and all the way to it being a place that will open at the end of the Land during the Exodus. You can choose which one to believe in."

The caravan moved away, leaving Stragif alone with his thoughts. Eventually, after hours of trial and error, leading only to errors and no success, Stragif sat at a bench in the plaza at the river's intersection. The sun made its procession across the sky. The morning had ended, and it was high noon.

"Excuse me," said a soft yet intense woman's voice. "Might I sit by your side?"

When Stragif looked at her, he saw a sparrow with perfectly treated feathers, but instead of the usual white, some of her feathers had a tremendous dark brown color with pieces of pitch black. Her face had some white feathers, though—so white, in fact, that not even the snow was so distinct in color. Everything about her was incoherent in some weird way.

"Of course, woo," Stragif said, too tired to hide the "woo," giving her some space to sit by his side.

For a moment, there was silence between them. The hydra flowing through the river, moving to the ocean, gave Stragif a nostalgic feeling. He was homesick.

"Did you know," the woman said after a minute of silence, "that we don't drink the hydra from this river here in the Kingdom?"

"No, I didn't— No. Wait. I do. Of course I do. I always drink it from somewhere else." he said. In his panic, he noticed that sections of her feathers were dirtied, not by sand or dust but by mud and tar—easy to spot as his disguise employed a similar technique.

"I always thought that the owls knew everything," she said after a quiet laugh. "You don't need to pretend. I don't think you would fool anyone."

"I'm sorry for trying, woo, but my friend is in dire need of help."

"Is it? Well, unless you can offer trade, us Sparrows are very protective of our land and the Aves that dwell in it. I don't think many would help."

"I know, woo. I felt it first hand."

"But please, don't think ill of us. We just follow the Way of the Aves far stronger than any other Order," she said.

"I know that, woo. I've heard the myths and legends from this place. I read many myself. Others were taught by my elders, and I listened to the old stories, but we didn't come here of our own volition. We came here because the Land guided us."

"What is it that you seek?" she asked, turning to Stragif with great interest in his story. "You seem so sad. I can't begin to imagine what happened."

"We search for Mount Kingdom Come, woo, for a way to help him out of sadness."

"But why would one walk a path with no destination, searching for a thing that can't be found beyond your own heart and devotion to the Way of the Aves?" she asked. "Mount Kingdom Come should be inside of you."

"You don't understand, woo. It has to be real. If it isn't, then what *is* Raven, truly?"

"So, his name is Raven? Isn't he your friend?"

"No, woo, he is my savior. He saved my daughters, and…" Stragif wanted to say more but didn't know how. How could you convince someone that a god fell from the sky and can't return? He wouldn't believe it himself.

"Bring him here before sundown," she demanded with precise words. "I might be able to procure help."

"I can't, woo. He can only travel at night."

"We, the Sparrows, can't break our vows. We only work during the day," she explained with a certain sadness.

"I can bring him during the night, woo, and tomorrow, you can help, correct?"

"I'm afraid I can't say I'll help for certain tomorrow…"

"Please, woo. You're the first person to listen to me. Help me. Help us!"

The female sparrow stood up from the bench and stared at the city, her eyes following the daily lives of the people in it. To Stragif's surprise, she quickly sang a strange, disconnected song unlike any other he had ever heard. She was a terrible singer.

"If he can't come here, then I shall go to him. Take me to your place," she said, turning towards him with decisive eyes.

"What? Woo? Are you not afraid of following me?"

"There are worse things that I fear. Your words might tell lies, but your eyes and actions show me the truth."

"Thank you, woo. Thank you…"

"Eloise," the sparrow said. "Call me Eloise."

Raven gulped down and then swiftly regurgitated the water provided by Eloise with a choking cough.

"I know it tastes horrible," Eloise lamented, "but it's pure hydra, taken from the ocean. Every sparrow drinks it."

"Thank you," Raven replied. "I shouldn't be doing such a thing when you're helping me."

"Don't worry," Eloise said, leaving some food on the cave's floor. "I shall return tomorrow night with more provisions. If you're feeling better, you might tell me a little more about the two of you and what led you to such disastrous consequences."

Raven wasn't feeling *slightly* better the next evening, but rather, he felt incredibly improved.

"Some of your minor bruises seem to have vanished," Eloise said after quickly checking Raven's body. She'd arrived way past the moon had reached its highest point.

"Why do you come so late, woo? I thought you Sparrows were all conscripted by your duty. Isn't it attuned to the day?"

"Yes," Eloise replied, her eyes moving away from his.

"You all seem so trapped by your duties," Raven observed. "One can only learn at night, the other can only live in the day. Why is that?

Aren't you all curious about what happens in between?" He needed to conjure all his strength to complete the question.

"Well, it's because the Creator demanded that of us, dear Raven." Eloise was taken aback, for such a question was unthinkable. "The Way of the Aves demands that of us; otherwise, the Land shall return to the Dark Years of Madness."

Eloise grabbed some hydra and poured it into Raven's mouth before continuing with a tale.

"You see, long ago, after the Creator made all the Land and all the Aves to inhabit it, he left, allowing us to live a perfect life in this self-sufficient world. And in such perfection came growth, for the Land provided what we needed. The weather was perfect for each ave Order, and we could enjoy our days in happiness." Eloise grabbed Raven's head, like a mother showing care for her child. "But that didn't last, for the more we grew, the more we needed to eat, and the Land couldn't provide enough in a timely manner. In due time, the Aves fell to madness, trying to find ways to keep their Orders alive. Two Orders did the unthinkable: the Crows, who were incredibly smart, capable of seeing ahead of them, and the Gaizers, strong Aves with a touch of darkness in them, for they were made for the night. They allied together to save their Orders.

"Such a collaboration drove many to famine, the sky was painted in black as they roamed. Every ave was eventually driven into madness. To prevent the Exodus from happening, the goddesses, Sunshine and Starlight, descended upon the Land to a place called Mount Kingdom Come and issued the Five Laws that every Order would have to abide by to restore the world to how it was."

"The Fifth Law, woo," Stragif added, "says that we must not join with another Family or Order, for doing so would open the way to the Exodus once again."

"I knew of the Laws," Raven said, "but not of their history. The First Law talks about the Land belonging to the Creator: Anything that is not his should not be accepted. The second talks about loving each other like you love yourself." Raven coughed a little, still in pain, trying to recall the other three laws.

"There will be no gain at the hands of another's loss is the third one," Eloise said

"The fourth, you proudly proclaimed once, woo: 'The Creator is the only one that gives life. He is the only one with the authority to take it,'" Stragif added.

"Later, after that, the Aves created The Ways of the Aves," Eloise continued, "wherein Kingdoms and their representatives were formed based on an Order or Family of ave, each with a duty to execute so that the Land can remain proper and in balance—"

Something stopped Eloise midway through her thought process, and without a single word, she vanished away in the night.

She returned the following night to find Raven even stronger, now capable of moving around.

"Tell me, Eloise, why do you break the duty of the Sparrows?" Raven asked.

"Our duty is to guard this sacred soil from the interjection of different lifestyles so that the birds, in their daily duty, can live a great and prosperous life."

"Seems quite vague to me," Raven replied, "and you did not answer my question."

"Tell me the reason why you're here, and I might tell you why I do what I do."

"You might not believe me, but I'm a god," Raven said, and as expected, Eloise clearly didn't believe him.

"A god? Can't you find a better lie?" she questioned him with sarcasm in her voice.

"But it's the truth. I disobeyed my partner, Starlight, who gave me instructions on how to behave, and in doing so, I was cast away from Murdek and trapped on the Land."

"Disobeyed?" Eloise muttered in a whisper to herself. "Do you think she hates you for doing so?" she promptly asked as if the words were trapped right under her tongue the whole time.

"No, I don't think so. I think she was sad as, when I fell, the last time I saw her face, she was shedding tears for me. I think I might have broken her heart in a way I can't truly understand."

"Tears? She cried for you? For your disobedience?" Eloise said, more like a question to herself than towards Raven.

"Are you alright?" Raven asked, noticing a single tear departing from Eloise's eyes.

"I'm sorry to the two of you. I've been untruthful regarding a lot of things, especially myself," Eloise replied, walking fast-paced in a circle.

She suddenly stopped.

"I'll help you. You'll reach Mount Kingdom Come. I know the way," Eloise said, grabbing Raven's hand.

"What, woo?" Stragif replied in shock.

"I told you, didn't I? Our duty is to protect this place, which guards the entrance to Mount Kingdom Come. My father has a key that allows passage into it. I'll ask him for help. He'll open the way for you. You're a god, after all, right?"

She ran towards the cave entrance, letting go of Raven.

"Wait, woo. You can't just leave us like that, Eloise," Stragif said, moving towards her.

"I'm not 'Eloise.' My name is Victoria," she proudly announced. "Father—" escaped her mouth, a word she clearly wanted to keep a secret as another tear ran down her face, reflecting the silver light of the moon. And then, she flew away.

"Victoria, woo?" Stragif questioned, moving his head. "Raven, I think we've been speaking with the Princess of the Sparrows this whole time."

Chapter 7

The Princess

At night, the Kingdom of the Sparrows always sits still in perpetual peace. The sound of crickets creates lasting echoes that proclaim that the day is past.

That night, Victoria soared across the forest glades, effortlessly moving between the trees. Her eyes were guided by the moonlight passing through the foliage, no different from when the sunshine passed between the clouds on an overcast day. In the distance, the river intersection at the capital's center glimmered in a silver color, guiding her path.

A sad song echoed from the depths of the forest—an unorganized rhythmic thing, lacking reason or meaning.

What? At this time? She was full of questions as she searched for the source of the missing harmony, confused as to why she would be hearing it at this time.

She glided down towards it, reaching a place where the moonlight could not touch, and hiding in the shadows, a little ave sang his dramatic tune.

"Vic," the little one called when she approached, "I knew you'd be around."

"Why are you here at this time? If they catch you…"

"You know they won't," he proudly said. "That's why you're here now."

She knew she couldn't go against his logic; Sparrows would be too proud to work in the night and break their perfect order—a perfect blind spot for her escapades.

"And what about other dangers?" Victoria questioned him, noticing a smudge of the black paint from her feathers sticking to the little hatchling's white ones. "Don't make me say it again: *Don't* follow me into the night."

"But I wasn't following you! I mean, I was, but I wasn't either!" he said in confusion. "My mom, she is so… I don't know. She is like your dad. I don't like her. I want to fly away and…" But he trailed off, noticing Victoria's angry eyes devouring his soul.

"Listen," she said, kneeling to reach him, "I'm appreciative of your help with the guards during the day, but I don't want you to get the wrong impression. Your parents are very important, and I'm sure they care about you."

Her mind was filled with distinctive images, some of her father's requesting something impossible from her. In others, she saw Raven proclaiming the care of his elder. They flashed intermittently, collapsing in a mess of strange feelings.

"So, why do you keep running away from yours?" the little one asked impatiently.

"I don't know," she said, watching his face contort itself, denoting confusion. "The harsh truth is that I still don't yet know why I do the things I do. All I know is that they are my emotions and actions, they don't need to be yours."

"But I thought we were… What was the word again?"

"Accomplices?" she replied with a smile.

"Yes, that thing. Secret songs and all that. Doesn't it mean we should act together?"

"It just means you believe in me, not that you are me."

He looked deeply into her eyes with even more confusion. *Where was this passage from again?* she asked herself, recalling that she'd once read her last phrase in a philosophy book. *Not that I ever cared, but still, it came in handy now.*

The gleaming light from the river vanished, reflecting the moon's vanishing act as it hid behind a cloud traveling high up in the sky. The hatchling's eyes widened in fear.

"What is that?" he asked, pointing towards something lurking behind Victoria.

When she turned to see it, two blue eyes hid themselves among the foliage of the tallest tree. Her eyes were not made for the darkness of the night, and without the moon's guidance, there was very little she could make out besides the size of the enormous ave watching them.

Instinctively, she pushed the boy all the way behind her and assumed a defensive position.

"I don't know what or who you are, but I don't fear you," she said in a defiant tone. It was mostly true; her heartbeat had increased, but in a way, that was only nature's method of preparing her for a fight or flight, not a means to cripple her under uncontrollable actions.

"Why not? Everyone but you fears me. Don't you see me as a monster?" the giant ave spoke in a feminine voice with no joy.

"I'm sorry?" Victoria replied in surprise. She did not expect such a response, and she did not know how to give an answer. "Who are you?"

"I wish I knew that, too. Does everyone truly know who they are?" the blue-eyed ave replied, throwing back another question.

"I mean, yes," Victoria replied. "I don't think there is—"

But the hatchling was acting like me, she interrupted herself, diving into deep thought. *Does he know who he is?*

"We are the figures of our elders," Victoria continued after her own interruption, thinking back to the philosophy text she had had to read once on her father's orders. *Is that true, though?* she asked herself, doubting her own words immediately after speaking them.

"Elders? Like parents? I've never met mine," the dark ave replied in sorrow.

The moonlight drew a line in the darkness, slowly increasing its reach as the clouds finally passed by it, allowing all its silver splendor to shine and touch the land. Before it could reach the tallest tree, where the blue-eyed ave resided, she took flight, each flap of her enormous wings creating a tempest of wind.

When the light finally reached the place where she had been, nothing was there but the afterimage inside Victoria's mind.

"Who was that?" the hatchling questioned.

"I don't know," Victoria replied with honesty. "You see, little one, that is why we shouldn't walk in the dark. Let's go back home before your mom notices you vanished."

Or my father…

"Where were you, Victoria?" the King of the Sparrows spoke. The throne room was brilliant in the middle of the dark, illuminated by fireplaces that acted as fake suns to keep the place drowning in perpetual light.

"Studying as thou ordered," Victoria replied in a polite monotone.

"No husband will ever want you, for your escapades at night bring shame to a Sparrow's duty," the king said. He could bring the world to a tremble with his voice without the need to raise it a bit.

"But, dear Father—I mean, Lord Reemus—this conversation avails us naught. We lavish far too much time articulating over it," Victoria replied. Her voice had remained calm, and yet, a fierce determination escaped through her words.

"Nay, Princess Victoria. We shall end this charade tonight," Lord Reemus said, arranging himself on the throne. He wore a long yellow cape tied around his neck with a precise knot on a red rope. "Look at your state, your feathers disturbed like an ave whose duty is to clean the Land, not to rule and protect it," He showed the adorning patterns designed on his cape, three symbols representing the ocean's hydra, the green lands, and the mountains around them.

"Forgive me, Lord Reemus, but you talk of duty, and yet, you decide to pass judgment over me in the night when you and your guards should be deeply asleep. To judge me is but a farce! The Order of the Sparrows deserves to know of it."

"Silent, child!" Lord Reemus shouted. "I pray that the Creator and the Gods of Birds forgive my indiscretion. I set this palace abundant with light to trick the moonlight and its watchful gaze. Why do I do such things? To erase, once and for all, this: the demise you bring upon us by taking such callous actions."

"You're just doing it for yourself, Father…"

"In this court, you call me by my title, Princess Victoria," Lord Reemus imposed.

"What am I to you? The princess? Or your *daughter*? Don't you want to see me happy?"

"Under the Order, you're the Princess of the Sparrows—she who shall carry the duty of protecting Mount Kingdom Come. Outside of it, you're the daughter I love and would sacrifice the world for, but for my daughter Victoria, not for this ave called Eloise."

"You know of that?" Victoria said, surprised.

"I know much and more of what you do and how you enlist the new hatchlings to play your games and distract the guards. This shall be over soon, though. Tell me, how are your studies in philosophy and history going?"

"They are complete as far as the professors tell me. I've read all the tomes available in this castle."

"I'm surprised that you managed to find the time to read while soaring abroad," Lord Reemus replied. "But I'm glad such a thing happened. Tomorrow, you and I shall look for your future husband. Are we in agreement? Or would thou rather see the Exodus falling upon us all?"

I can't tell him about Raven in this situation. He'll think I'm trying to trick him. "Thou art the Lord, the guiding light that protects the Land," Victoria said while bowing, a common phrase in the nobility used to signify the end of a conversation.

"Don't leave this court until we are done, Princess!" Lord Reemus shouted.

"I understood you the first time..." Victoria said, leaving the room, but before she reached the entrance arches, she stopped and turned back to ask a simple question. "Father, would you cry for me if I disobeyed you beyond your beliefs?" Victoria asked, throwing away all the fancy words and titles. In her mind, Raven's story echoed in a chamber with nothing but every wrongdoing she had ever done.

Lord Reemus seemed to be taken aback by such a question, as he did not respond straight away. Victoria wondered where his mind went.

"I'm sorry, Lord Reemus," Victoria finally said, breaking the silence. "Mine words were unnecessary," she completed, leaving the room.

"There is no parent in this world that would not cry for its hatchling," he finally said, but Victoria was too far away to ever hear it.

"You don't need to do this, Dexter," Victoria said to one of the Royal Guards as she witnessed him bar the windows of her room.

"Those are Lord Reemus's instructions," George interjected from across the room. "We can't afford to keep the Order awake the whole night watching you."

"Couldn't you two use the head the Creator gave you to think for yourselves, for once?" Victoria questioned them.

"It's not in my place to think beyond the Order's duties and the Lord's command," Dexter replied, shutting down the last window in the room. "Now, do us all a favor and have a good night's sleep." Dexter closed her room's door as the two guards walked out. The sound of a key sliding the lock shut resounded across the palace hallways, making certain that, for the night, Victoria wouldn't leave.

She took the time she had to clean her feathers, removing the mud and tar she'd used to paint them. She had grown so used to the colors that she felt uneasy looking at the mirror in her room, seeing a different person staring back at her. Deep down, though, she knew that person staring back was Princess Victoria—the real her, not Eloise.

I don't want to hide anymore, she told herself, dressing up in different red and yellow fashionable clothes adorned with the triple symbol of the crown. *Eloise must go.*

She paced across the room, trying to settle herself for sleep, but her thoughts kept her awake. The idea of a god falling from the sky seemed so out there, so distant from reality, that she might as well be dreaming. She knew that Raven and Stragif lacked evidence, but she couldn't ignore the possibility that they were telling the truth. Or rather, she didn't want to ignore it, she wanted to believe it. More than anything, she wanted to believe that her mundane, boring days would come to an end if a god walked on the Land, changing the Order of the Aves forever.

Could Raven do it? Could he undo all of this?

She flipped through the pages of books painstakingly written by the greatest Owls to have ever lived. Each letter was like a masterpiece brushed in black and red strokes; in all likelihood, it took longer for a page to be written in such a beautiful way than it took her to read the whole book.

"We are the figures of our elders," Victoria whispered as she caught a glimpse of it next to a painting in the final pages of the book. The image depicted white feathered elder Aves teaching language, drawing, and culture and feeding their young ones, who, in turn, were teaching their hatchlings. Despite the size difference, the Aves were depicted with the same colors, faces, and postures, as if they were the same being across generations. The whole scene took place on a dark red background, and the Aves were trapped inside circles where the terms "Kingdom," "Lord," "Order," and "Family" encapsulated them all.

Elders love their younglings, do they not? So much so that they waste their whole life teaching them, Victoria found herself deep in thought. *Surely, my father loves me. He gave me all of this, and he thinks about my future all the time. Surely, he does.*

Suddenly, a burning passion flickered inside her heart. *He will forgive me, just like Starlight will certainly forgive Raven,* she found herself thinking, flipping the pages of another tome—a novel Lord Reemus used to read to her at bedtime.

In no time, she found what she was looking for and put herself into action, building a contraption similar to the one the heroine in the story uses to escape the prison she finds herself in.

The Key to the Mount should be in the depths of the Passage Halls, she told herself, breaking the lock of the door open.

She looked outside, and as predicted, no sparrow dared to be awake at this time. She took her leave, stepping out into the forbidden.

All I need to do is steal the key to Mount Kingdom. Come and deliver it to Raven. My father doesn't need to know, she told herself, strolling in silence through the tranquil halls of the Palace, not disguised as Eloise but as the true person she had always been: Princess Victoria of the Kingdom of the Sparrows.

CHAPTER 8

The Prisoner

Victoria began her dance down the hallways of the palace, tiptoeing on her feet like an air ballerina from the flamingos' performance tents to gently touch the ground. She didn't think she was as graceful as such a prestigious ave, but she tried to recall her classes from the days of yore. Her coat made of leAves wasn't the best to muffle movement, but it could carry multiple things and hide her in dark places, so its use was more than justified.

The halls surrounding her were magnificently drowning in darkness, and not a single soul was to be seen walking around, making it even easier to slide between the innocuous doors without having to find an excuse as to where she was going—a freedom the daylife never truly allowed.

Past the throne room, though, Victoria found herself inside the Hall of the Eternal Sun, the name taken from the eternally lit torches—a brilliant excuse created by the Sparrows to justify heavy guard duty during the night for the most sacred item they held dear: the passage where the Key to Mount Kingdom Come resided.

From here on, the Restless Watchers will be moving out and about. How am I to evade them? She moved past sacred inscriptions in the walls towards a single, lonely cedar door.

She approached the handle, holding her breath, for she knew that once she turned it open, there would be no turning back—no lie she could concoct would be large enough to justify what she was about to do. Treason of the highest level against the Order of the Sparrows would only lead her towards a singular destination: the end of her life for disturbing the Way of the Aves.

She opened the door, taking a peek inside. The once-linear hallway now broke itself in two different directions, forming a circular corridor with windows to an interior garden. No sunlight could come in— the roof had to be inaccessible—so instead of the intense greenery that surrounded the palace and the city, the place had grown purple plants such as the purple-leaved coleus; the intense, almost pink toad lilies; or the magnificent yet fragile hellebores.

Watching the flowers as one would watch their hatchlings, in the middle of a crowded space, two sparrows stood in guard, wearing long sets of golden armor that were extremely reflective, making the eternally lit torches shine off them as if they were the blazing sun themselves.

Through the window, on the other side of the round corridor where both passages met, Victoria could see another guard patrolling. His march would eventually catch up to her if she didn't move.

But where do I go now? Any direction I move, a guard will spot me…

Victoria took, from under her wings, the tar she normally used to disguise her snowy feathers. She enveloped some leAves with it, making little bombs.

They'll figure out it was me once they see the tar. Hopefully, once Father sees that Raven is a god, he'll forgive me.

She took aim at the closest torch, preparing to paint it black and plunge the place into darkness.

But darkness decided to arrive before her actions, for as all the torches were suddenly put out at once, the braziers gave off only the light of the simple embers that were left.

"What was that? Has the night downed on us?" she heard one of the guards comment. "Quick," another one shouted. "If we don't relight it, we'll be committing a sin against the Order," he said as the wind picked up.

The wind touched the tip of her wings, moving her coat around. It moved in a strange way, like no wind she had ever witnessed, for this one seemed to curve and bend following the corridor's path. And so, she followed it.

She noticed the patrolling guard's armor clicks echoing from the other side of the corridor and the two other guards moving about in the garden in a direction completely opposite to hers.

The wind is truly guiding me. It is like the legends. Is the Land showing me the way? Her faith in Raven's story grew stronger. *The Land wanted me to reach the key,* she reassured herself.

She passed through another set of doors, all unlocked, with hallways submerged in pitch black. She could hear the guards, but they couldn't hear her, they couldn't see her, and if one ever got close to her, the wind would blow them away, making them change directions.

At last, she found herself in the Chamber of Providence, where the Key resided on a pedestal under the watch of not a sparrow but a different ave: an owl. The darkness wouldn't be her friend there.

Owls were intriguing creatures; beyond the ones that lived in the Kingdom of the Owls, their Order spread far and wide, the smartest of them living luxurious lives as members of the courts in the multiple Kingdoms and Orders spread across the Land, dutifully resigned to teach and record the history of the high aristocracy. The owl residing in the Kingdom of the Sparrows once was Victoria's teacher as the sun covered the early morning sky, but that owl was the protector of the Kingdom's greatest treasure once the moon took rise above the horizon.

Hydra met Victoria's feet as soon as she stepped in. The entire place seemed as if it had been sunk by an invader; the shapes of the pillars and rocks that were submerged indicated that the substance didn't belong there. For each movement Victoria made, the hydra responded in kind with a gracious sound similar to a rock falling into a pond, and for one with good hearing, her presence would be noticed.

Victoria stopped in place, holding her breath, the sound of the hydra moving further down in the round announcing another being moving about.

"This is unprecedeeented," she heard, deep in the chamber. The long enunciation of the final word triggered the familiar and announced the obvious to Victoria: This was her old teacher speaking. "I've never seen hydra inside such a plaaace. I have to recooord it."

He doesn't seem to have noticed me yet. Was this so sudden?

The wind returned to its sentience state, moving hydra left and right, crashing it like the ocean's wAves crash against the beach. Victoria used the opportunity to move about towards a dead brazier emitting a faded ember and letting its final flames be shown to the world.

Victoria took the dry leAves from her attire and threw them inside the brazier. She blew on it. The wind, picking up on her plan, moved away from it, allowing the intensity of the ember to grow, and soon enough, fire was born. The wind returned towards her and carried the embers, lighting the other braziers around the room.

The resplendent colors reflected on the hydra, illuminating the room as if the sun had brightened the morning with midday light— brighter than it needed to be.

"My eeeyes," Victoria's master cried. "They burn! What is happening here? Is this the Laaand? Is that you, Creator?"

I wonder that, too, Victoria thought, moving towards the pedestal where a strange engraved key rested, the shape more triangular than she expected.

Her eyes, for the first time, took the chance to see the room. Unlike the garden before, this place was devoid of any life. There were no paintings on the wall like the ones surrounding the castle; the triple insignia of the Sparrows was missing. There was just a place cut into the bedrock with some braziers around.

Victoria didn't dwell for too long inside it. She took the Key and exited as fast as she could.

What a strange place, she thought to herself as she rushed across the palace hallways back to her safe haven, where all sparrows would be asleep. *Didn't Father tell me that, during the day, braziers were lit inside that room for the sparrows that would watch over their key while my master rested? We are hours into the night now. How could the embers still be strong after so many hours?*

Regardless of the answer, Victoria admitted nothing tonight made much sense; the wind, the hydra, the braziers, they all worked in her favor as if ordained by the Creator to do so. *Raven must be a God of Birds. That is the only explanation.*

Victoria used her lockpicking skills to open a window and took flight away from the castle. Although her heart beat in a pattern that she thought to be out of synchronicity, her mind was at ease. She knew that she'd just done something incredibly wrong, and yet, she felt free from any burden that might carry. She was a prisoner no longer.

"What an intriguing object, woo," Stragif said, examining the Key Victoria had brought. "And you mentioned the place is protected by an owl?"

"Yes, it is. My master who taught me many things about the world."

"I've never heard of such a duty inside our Order, woo," Stragif shook his head.

"The Land is full of secrets," Raven commented, moving around the little cave, "as was Murdek. Even I didn't know of it all."

"Are you feeling better?" Victoria asked, seeing the Phoenix move around.

"I should be able to fly," Raven replied. "Not sure for how long, but I feel strong."

Victoria couldn't help but notice that Raven had regrown all his feathers, and his skin burns had vanished completely. Certainly, a miracle must have happened there. "Is it common?" she asked. "For a god to heal this fast? Honestly, I never thought one could be damaged in the first place."

"It's certainly uncommon, woo. I recall your bruises lasting forever back in the Kingdom of the Owls. Even after the incident with the hydra in the mountains, you had burned feathers for days to come."

"Hydra?" Victoria asked, recalling the night's recent incident. "Did something strange happen with it? I'm just asking because I had some trouble with it tonight. The room my master protected was filled with it, and the wind also acted strangely, as if it was alive and guiding me."

"I was told by Starlight that I was born to command the winds and the hydra of the world," Raven said. "Since I touched the star, though, my powers over them seem to come and go as they please. At times, I am even stronger than I used to be. In the mountains, I could see the hydra flowing underground like a river no one knew about."

"Do you think your powers were guiding me?" Victoria asked.

"Or could it be the Land moving itself to allow Raven to reach Mount Kingdom Come, woo. There are some truths to the stories, aren't there?" Stragif questioned Victoria.

"I know only that my Order protects the way, and every Lord in every Kingdom knows of this, but beyond that, I can only guess," Victoria replies. "For the common folk, this might be how they reach it, but I have never heard of it ever happening."

"And how does this open the way?" Raven asked. "Surely, a mountain can't be hidden inside a cave or a palace, can it?"

"There is a place called the Great Frontier, where the ocean, the desert, the mountain, and the forest meet one another. In that place, the pedestal where the Key goes is hidden. Beyond that, I'm afraid I don't know. I've never been to Mount Kingdom Come. I know my father has been there once, though, so I'm certain this is the procedure."

"Lord Reemus visited the sacred place, woo? What purpose could he have with the God of Birds?" Stragif asked, waiting for no answer as he knew Victoria wouldn't know, and an answer he didn't get.

"Let's not waste our time here anymore," Raven suggested. "They are bound to begin a search for this key as soon as morning comes, so we better get moving." "The second I reach the gates of Murdek once again," Raven continued, speaking to Victoria, "I shall tell your father and Starlight of your good deeds. He certainly will protect you, as every parent does."

The place where all types of life met—where the fauna of the forest met its end in the dry desert, where the arid mountain soil touched the ocean's breeze and sea hydra splashed on its tall cliffs—was a sight to behold.

The trip there wasn't the fastest. Raven still had some difficulty flapping his wings, but the intrepid trio managed to reach the place before sunrise.

If possible, I'd love to keep what happens with me when the sun comes up away from her sight, Raven told himself. *I don't want people believing I'm weak. I don't want to be seen as a weak God of Birds.*

From afar, they could already see a strange structure leading to the interior of a cave by the desert's wayside. As a casual passerby, they would see nothing more than yellow rocks sculpted by the desert's sand and the ocean's breeze, but now that he knew something was there, their triangular shape made more sense.

They landed in front of the cave, Raven's feet touching the hot desert sand, triggering in him some memories he'd rather forget. He moved on fast, stepping inside the cave, where the cold rock made him feel far better. Memories of his days in the Kingdom of the Owls' large cave surfaced in his mind.

Inside, leAves carried by the wind from the forest had grown dry, and sea hydra had managed to find its way in, using underground tunnels to create giant lakes in the vast, open cave sections.

"Do sparrows tend to wake up early, woo?" Stragif asked Victoria as they traveled, flying through chambers so large, they could see neither the bottom nor the top.

"No, not at this time, at least. Maybe, a little before the sunrise," Victoria replied, her eyes trying to see a way forward in the pitch-black darkness—far more a struggle than during her own little adventure inside the palace walls.

"It certainly was a caravan then, woo," Stragif mused. "I saw multiple light sources moving across the forest.

"It can't be my father, that is for sure. He wouldn't dare follow me in the night and break his vows.".

Raven couldn't believe it, but the further they kept going inside the cave, the darker it felt. *How can darkness be so intense?*

"I shall guide us, woo," Stragif said.

The sound of waterfalls echoed in the large chamber, making it hard to hear. They had a unique smell; the hydra wasn't fresh, but instead, it contained salt. The entire cave system was filled with ancient ruins—pillars, poles, and columns stretching from the unseen bottom; they showed that once, at least, the Aves of yore had traveled across this place so constantly that they built structures around it.

They kept moving further into the cave system for what seemed to be an eternity. *How deep in the mountains could we be?* Raven caught himself thinking from time to time.

A sad song was sung somewhere within. The chorus added a melody out of harmony to the sound of the waterfall. Victoria ceased her movements. Her wings flapped, but she stood still in place while her head moved out and about, searching for something.

"Is something wrong?" Raven asked her.

"Stragif, can you see a sparrow hatchling anywhere?" Victoria asked, her voice trembling.

"Why would a hatchling be here, woo? I don't see anyone but us here."

Victoria quickly changed her stance, her wings flapping diagonally, her movements taking her away from them. "Where are you?" she shouted, her words mixing in the ever-growing echo chamber. "Where are—"

Light everlasting broke inside the room. Raven's eyes burned for a second before adjusting to the new sight. He could finally see a part of the walls and waterfalls but try though he might, even with such abundant light, neither ceiling nor ground could he gaze, so colossal was the place he found himself in.

"George, stop!" Victoria shouted, but when Raven turned around to see what was happening, Stragif had passed out, trapped between the claws of a sparrow dressed in a soldier's armor.

"Capture the Stranger alive," demanded an authoritarian voice, strong and powerful. He held, by his side, a little sparrow and was protected by another sparrow dressed in perfect shining armor.

"Father, please, you don't understand," Victoria pledged.

"I see perfectly well. All the pieces fit together. He was the one that made thee into Eloise," Lord Reemus proclaimed. "But don't fret, Victoria, I do understand thy situation. All shall hear how he made you carry out such vile actions."

"He isn't the Stranger, Father," she cried, but he couldn't hear.

"We shall speak of this later, Eloise," Lord Reemus said. Victoria's face broke in despair.

The soldier by his side flew towards Raven, revealing a spear hidden beneath his wings. Raven thought of saying something, but what could he say when a sharp object moved towards him at such a fierce speed? The last time he tried to talk, the Mountain Eagles had attacked him regardless.

And so, he made the only reliable decision and thrust himself forward, initiating a deep dive, hoping the place truly didn't possess a floor or that, at least, it wouldn't be too close to him.

The spear pierced through him, and the claws grabbed Raven with such power that the Stranger in the forest seemed weak in comparison. But Raven would not give up so fast. He used all his strength to keep on a flight trajectory, pulling the soldier with him.

"Dexter, he isn't who you think he is," Victoria tried to call the knight to reason.

"Or maybe you're the one that doesn't know who he is," George retorted. "Do you believe in others that easily?"

"What do you mean? Do you know something I don't?"

Raven kept his flight inside the eternal chamber, bleeding from the place where the spear pierced him.

"I'd rather you stop now before you die," Dexter told him. "All we want is to capture you."

"No, you won't stop me," Raven screamed. "I'll return home."

"Return home," Lord Reemus repeated after Raven. "So, it's really you, dark ave."

"Father, what is going on! Do you know something I don't?" Victoria begged for an answer with her voice full of power. But she heard nothing back. She received only a glimpse of his eyes analyzing her.

Raven attempted to call the winds, trying to conjure the powers he had manifested once before when he and the Stranger first fought, but to no avail, for the wind seemed to ignore him.

Devoid of options, Raven tried one final movement and crashed against one of the waterfalls in the hopes Dexter would let go of him. The sea hydra poured inside his spear wound, and the salt made it burn. Yet, that was all he accomplished, for Dexter remained attached to him.

The last thing Raven saw was something that, by now, he had grown used to as he crashed against a solid surface from high in space. This time, though, instead of hitting the floor and creating a crater, the cave's dirty wall finally met him face-to-face.

He saw a darkness far greater than the depths he found himself in.

"Father, why don't you listen to me?" Victoria cried.

"This isn't thine duty to know. This is mine to correct a judgment long overdue," Lord Reemus said.

CHAPTER 9

The Great Council of Birds

There was no moon nor sunlight that could reach Raven deep inside the dungeon. If not for the tiny gap between the bars that allowed food to be delivered to him, he would think even air couldn't reach him.

Most of the hours, he would be alone with his thoughts, occasionally visited by the guard bringing him food and water. Stragif was nowhere to be seen. Victoria was a ghostly image in his mind. Thankfully, at least, the spear cut had completely vanished, and with each passing day, Raven grew ever stronger.

Something in this Kingdom gives me strength? Is it the Mount? Raven pondered.

A plate with some fruits came in through the porthole, and the guard quickly switched it for the old plate and hydra. The single light, coming from a candlestick over a table in the outside corridor, brightened the prison cell slightly better for a couple of seconds, only for the partial darkness to creep in once again.

"Can you tell me how long I've been here?" Raven asked the guard.

"Long enough," the sparrow replied curtly.

"Please, let me at least know this," Raven begged.

"You terrorized the Land, creature. Many families of Aves were destroyed by you. There is nothing you deserve to know."

"I've told you all, I'm not this monster you mistake me for."

"Have you taken a look at yourself?" the guard bitterly replied. "There is not a single other ave with your complexion. You're a defect in this world." The guard kicked the porthole, causing a reverberation that hit the plate of fruits, scattering them across the dirty floor.

For every Stragif I meet, a Stranger comes by. For every beautiful forest I pass, a desert rises. For the peaceful moonlight, the day draws in anguish over my body. This Land is full of the best and worst. But not Murdek, that place was perfect.

Raven's thoughts absorbed him into his mind. Since the cramped space didn't even allow his wings to be open, his mind was the only place he could freely move. Even if the wind had decided to obey him once more, he knew he was so deep down somewhere strange that such a thing wouldn't be possible. Not even the wind would grace him in that place.

What seemed like weeks passed. Each day healed Raven's bruises and muscles. But at this point, it didn't truly matter; his soul had been broken by solitude.

"Tomorrow, thou shall testify against the monster," Lord Reemus declared from his throne.

"But my Lord," Victoria replied, "I told you many times, he is a God of Birds."

"You? 'Thou' is the proper pronoun. 'You' is used by the gutter of the Land. There shall be no further use of such language in this court of mine!" Lord Reemus reprimanded the young ave.

"No! I won't pretend anymore, Father! You yourself keep forgetting to use those stupid words from time to time," Victoria slapped back.

"All I want is the best for you, my daughter. Why can't you see?" he replied softly, exhaustion dripping from every word.

"So, why can't you trust me?" Victoria pledged back.

"How can your proposal possibly be accurate, my lady?" Dexter gently queried, standing to the right-hand side of the throne. "My spear pierced him just like any other ave. A god would have deflected it," he said, lifting his golden spear.

"My dear Victoria, for once in your life, listen to me. Testify against the creature. Tell them how he corrupted you and forced you into stealing the Key," Lord Reemus told her, not as a request but as a demand.

"I took the Key of my own volition, Father. No one instructed me to do so. Don't dare to lecture me on our duty as Sparrows—of what I should've done. That night, you also broke the vows of our Order by acting underneath the moon."

"Because I knew you'd do something stupid," he lashed out. "Do you think you could've escaped that easily? Do you think I'm a fool for not knowing you can unlock doors? I know the stories you love. I know the skills you have. I know the Aves you speak with. I know you better than anyone. I'm your father, after all. I let you run amok for far too long. I had to do something…"

"You planned everything that night? My escape and all?" Victoria asked.

"I did not plan for you to steal the Key, but to escape, yes, I did. We are all creatures of habit. I knew you would and that I could show you the error of your mistakes, once and for all. That such mistakes were so great, I did not expect."

"But you made mistakes yourself, didn't you? You said as much back inside the cave. What are you trying to atone for? How can you be so blind to not notice that everyone makes mistakes."

"That is where you are mistaken, Victoria. I do see the wrongdoings of the past, and I'm now trying to fix them. I just hope such clarity reaches you as well. Consequences will come for us all, sooner or later." Lord Reemus waved, and the doors inside the throne room opened. George proudly walked in carrying a little sparrow hatchling under his wings.

"Father, don't bring him into this! It was my fault he was involved," Victoria exclaimed, her eyes filled with sadness.

"You see, Victoria, your actions took us to this point. He is the consequence of your mistakes," Lord Reemus said. "Tomorrow, you shall get the chance to make things right and help little Timus return home."

Stragif could walk inside the palace library, but he couldn't fly or move fast enough as a ball and chain were strapped to his ankle.

The library was enormous—far larger than anything he had ever seen. Books, maps, telescopes, and even stone slabs with scriptures existed in harmony with one another inside this place, well organized in perfect roles, reachable not by stairs but through flying. Such a thing made this trove of knowledge inaccessible to him.

"How are your eyes, liiittle one?" asked an enormous white owl, flying down with a book from the furthest shelf. "The trick they pulled on you happened with me the same night. Princess Victoooria almost turned me blind."

"I feel better, woo. So, you devised the attack plan?" Stragif questioned.

"I merely suggeeested it after the fact. The plan had been set in motion earlier that evening by Lord Reeeeeemus himself."

So, this is a court Owl, so smart they can add pieces to a plan already in motion. Can my daughter truly reach such a place in life?

"Tell me, liiittle one, is the content of this book true?" the Master Owl, Grenfold, asked, showing Stragif his notebook.

"It is, woo. I have been doing my duty and recording my journey alongside the young god, Raven."

"If so, then the points don't connect to one anooother," Master Grenfold said, his face deeply in thought.

"What points, woo? Do you believe in what I wrote?" Stragif's voice filled with renewed hope.

"Of course I dooo. Our Order's duty is to record, not to fabricate. Even the deepest secrets are recorded somewhere. I did so myseeelf." Master Grenfold's eyes quickly read each page of Stragif's book.

"Please, tell me the points that are missing, woo," Stragif begged.

"This would be a story from not so long agooo, inside Mount Kingdom Come, and involving great Lords. If I tell youuu it, please reveal to me more about this Raven."

"I will woo. Please tell me more. What happened here?" Stragif's eyes were shining, for he was about to learn something new.

"There is a catch, liiittle one," the Master Owl said. "No matter what, you need to refrain from telling this tale tomorrooow at the Council. Doing so could bring us an onslaught," he finished with a cautelous voice.

"Of course, woo, I promise."

"No maaatter what," Master Grenfold added in an ominous sentence, "do not interfere with history. Watch it, and recooord it."

The great day had come. Raven was carried, with chains weighing his wings down, across corridors and hallways. Eventually, he was put inside some kind of transportation device and moved across a large distance in the middle of the night. That night was the first time Raven saw Murdek in the sky once again.

He rebelled, trying to move around and break free, but that availed to naught. Soon, the moon was once again out of view, and then, yellow stone corridors passed in front of him. He was so tired of walls.

The transport came to a full stop, and the wooden walls surrounding it fell, revealing bars shaped like steel frames. He was trapped inside a birdcage.

Like an exotic animal, the gaze of multiple birds—all sitting in a circle atop giant yellow and red stone thrones—fixed on him. A collective gasp escaped them. The running hydra, falling from the ceiling in artificial waterfalls, followed the round shape of the room, creating a river flow that wasn't loud enough to muffle the whispers. The room's ceiling made sure to contain the sound inside.

"Is it true, then?" someone said.

"This is atrocious—a sin of the greatest proportion against the Creator," another one proudly proclaimed.

"Why should we bother talking? We know what to do," a third one added to the gasps.

"Please, my friends, let's remain calm," Lord Reemus shouted. His voice had the providence of a god. Silence came in an instant.

"Are we starting already?" Lord Phoenici, a pink flamingo, asked. Unlike the other Lords present, he wasn't sitting on a throne but rather standing over it on a single leg. "Lord Corvix is missing, isn't he?"

"Not only him," Lord Raphus mentioned—a half-sized black dodo. "The Eagles and Gaizers are nowhere to be seen."

"Lord Corax and Lord Corvix sent servants apologizing for their absences," Lord Reemus said. "Lord Thebas abstained himself."

"Don't the Eagles have families nearby?" Lord Raphus added. "Surely, Lord Thebas would have sent the Mountain Eagles to the Council."

"He made the suggestion, but our Master Owl, Grenfold, mentioned that the creature had been in contact with the monster and might be under threat to speak in his favor," Lord Reemus responded. "We shall understand more of this creature's power later as we hear from a witness."

"Please, tell me," Lord Saucerottia, an indigo hummingbird, said, zapping through the words as if they were a single tweet. "Which Family or Order does he belong to?" He quickly flitted from place to place across the room.

"Indeed," Lord Phoenici said. His vocal pronunciation had a royal flow, even when uttering only a single word. "Lord Grimald, could you specify it for us?"

"Try as I might," Lord Grimald—an old owl of unique, perfect white and tinted red feathers—responded, "I can't seem to recall any creature that fits the one I see in front of me." His voice was rough and deep, a symptom of age.

"So, it is as I feared," Lord Reemus said. "My Master Owl, Grenfold, has spent the past few weeks, upon my instruction, cross-checking books in search of this ave's Family and Order. But the search bore no results," he finished in a dramatic manner.

"Tell us, monster, who are your parents?" exclaimed a Lord Phastos.

"I'm a Phoenix, born in Murdek from the silver egg of the JuJuRae. I'm the God of the Night, partner to Starlight, the Goddess of the Moon," proclaimed Raven proudly, even though he found himself behind bars.

"Do you take us for fools?" Lord Grimald said in protest after another collective gasp. "Do not say such stupid things."

"You all know what that means, don't you?" Lord Reemus added in a dramatic totality.

The Aves exchanged glances with one another, judging each Order one by one.

"Which Order broke the Way?" the rooster demanded. "Tell us, and we shall kill them!"

"I concur! Interspecies acts are forbidden. Would they dare bring the Exodus upon us all?" the emu complained.

"Calm down, my friends," Lord Reemus announced. Silence fell in the room in a single instant. "Let's not try to kill each other for nothing, for that would be calling the Exodus upon us all, don't you think? Turning brother against brother, Family, and Orders against themselves. Such turmoil shall not pass."

"I assure you, I don't intend to deceive anyone," Raven said, "I'm truly from Murdek. Starlight is my partner."

Once again, the room found itself lost to chaos. But silence returned no sooner than when a golden spear hit the floor three times, announcing the entrance of someone of high importance.

Victoria didn't fly into the council, she walked in with her head hanging low. She wasn't chained, but her feet moved as if they carried the weight of the Land above them. Stragif accompanied her, both being escorted in by George, carrying a little sparrow sleeping in his arms.

"Eloise," Raven called for Victoria. "Please, explain it all to them. You trusted me, didn't you?"

But Victoria didn't reply.

"I'm sure that, by now, you all have heard the rumors," Lord Reemus said, "of the misdoings of my daughter. This 'Eloise,' as he calls her, is a fabrication of this monster's evil power. He is the Exodus incarnated!"

"Stragif, please, help me! You saw me when I fell from the sky in a rainbow."

"Lord Reemus, please listen to me, woo," Stragif said, his voice low so no one else could hear. "You're making a mistake, and sooner or later, the truth will come out."

"I don't know what you know, owl," Reemus responded. "This is the first step to cleaning my wings and unburdening them of my mistake."

"Can't you count, woo? Surely, you recall—"

"See, my friends," Lord Reemus suddenly proclaimed. "This monster's influence is so great that he sent one of his minions to convince me otherwise. But my faith is stronger!"

"No, woo! Surely, Lord Grimald recorded the night when a rainbow fell in the Kingdom of the Owls and illuminated the sky!"

"Of course we did," Lord Grimald replied. "It was nothing but a shooting star, my scholars told me."

"That is because none of you ever dared to check in the first place," Stragif shouted, no "woo" in sight.

"Do you dare to suggest we haven't been doing our duty?" Lord Grimald boomed. The depth of his voice sounded like a roar.

"I dare to say you never cared to leave your easy lives inside the castles and courts. "The ones that came to watch him were too afraid to approach. Even I made the mistake of leaving a fellow ave behind, lonely in a strange place he'd never seen before."

"Why would the Owls be avoiding their duty?" Lord Phastos asked.

"The monster resided for years in the Kingdom of the Owls, didn't it?" came Lord Phoenici.

"It stands to reason, then, that the Owls are the betrayers. His feathers are as gray as a normal Owl," zapped Lord Saucerottia.

"So, that is why they've been slacking on their duties?" Lord Raphus pondered.

"Calm down, my friends. Can you see it now? The pervasive nature of the creature—his powers tearing us apart," Lord Reemus said, silencing the room as usual. "He aims to disperse us, and we shall not let him do so."

"But Lord Reemus…" said a red and yellow parrot. "Lord Reemus knows he has to be born of someone. He *has* to be born of *someone…*"

"Victoria, please tell us: Where did this ave truly come from?" Lord Reemus asked politely.

Victoria felt silent, her eyes deep with sadness. George approached her, allowing Timus to fall under her gaze.

"Victoria?" Lord Reemus said with a long pause. "Or should I call you 'Eloise'?"

Every single eye in the room fell on her.

"He… He was born in Murdek, as… as a God of the Night…" she said reluctantly.

"Victoria, that is not what you told me last night," Lord Reemus clipped.

"Why are you doing this?" protested Stragif. "You won't save the Orders unless you tell them the truth."

"The truth?" Victoria suddenly snapped. "Do you know the truth? You knew it all along."

"I told you, my daughter, they've been manipulating you," Lord Reemus said before Stragif could reply.

"Tell me, Stragif. Tell me the truth," Victoria begged. "Why is my father doing this? How can Raven's death save the Way of the Aves?"

Stragif wanted to reply to her. He opened his beak, preparing the words to speak out, but he didn't. "Sorry, woo, only your father can say. If I do so myself, the Path to the Exodus might open," Stragif said in defeat.

"Victoria, don't waste our time anymore," Lord Reemus requested, his voice seeming to crack for an instant.

He doesn't want her to lie. Why is he so deadlocked into doing this? Raven thought. *Stragif, do you really know the truth? Have you been keeping it away from me?*

"No! I'm tired of you all and your stupid Orders and Rules," Victoria screamed, breaking Raven's thoughts. "You're my father. Why are you doing this?" she asked, but she didn't stay to hear the answer, taking flight as soon as the final word was spoken, leaving little Timus behind in George's arm.

"Apologies for this display," Lord Reemus said. His voice had a dark timbre underneath the certain tone. "As you see, the monster's powers corrupt far and deep. Even the great Sparrows can fall under its spell."

"No bird I have ever seen has such a skill," Lord Grimald said.

"That is because this creature is not a bird of the Land but rather a creation of the Exodus itself," Lord Reemus avowed. "He belongs to no Order, no Family, no Kingdom, no land. His very existence is simply meant to drive us down. And let it be known, once we deal with this one, there will be much more to do to strengthen our bonds again."

Lord Reemus took a minute of silence before continuing. The room waited for his guidance, too shocked to say anything. Their minds are broken by such a revelation. "Raise your wings towards the Creator's sky, those who are of a single mind and believe, just as I do, that erasing a being that terrorized the Land for so long is the true path to avoiding the Exodus."

And without hesitation, every wing in the room but Stragif and Timus's were raised towards the sky.

This Land is so repugnant. Why would they do such a thing? Why can't they listen? "Stragif," Raven shouted, "please, tell them the truth you know. Please, save me, my friend. I can't do it alone!"

'I'm sorry, Raven. I'll find another way, woo, but saying this, here and now, will lead only to a worse outcome."

"Worse than my death? The death of a god?"

"It's settled then," Lord Reemus proclaimed. "A death sentence it is."

All the Lords applauded, cheering together in unison, "The monster will finally be gone."

CHAPTER 10

Death Sentence

Raven found himself back inside the barely illuminated dungeon cell that he'd spent what seemed like months inside. Being in the dark for so long made him strangely miss the daylight.

The light outside his cell flickered, revealing a moving shadow of an ave covered in a cape approaching.

"Eloise," Raven exclaimed, recognizing the silhouette.

"I'm afraid not," the voice under the robes replied. Raven didn't need to see the face lying underneath to know who it was, for his words had sentenced him to death.

"What are you doing here? Don't you think you've done me enough harm already? Or are you here to laugh at me even more?" Raven said with repugnance.

"I'm here to apologize to you," Lord Reemus said, "and to let you know that I shall ensure to hide your siblings, if possible, and keep them safe."

"I don't have siblings. As I told you, I was born from a single silver egg of the JuJuRae on Murdek," his words emerged harshly.

"Did something else happen to the other eggs, then? I don't truly recall much after the meeting with Sunshine and Starlight," Lord Reemus pondered in the darkness. The flames' movement made his face under the robe shadowy and untrustworthy—not that Raven had any trust in the ave left.

"You've met Starlight? How? Call her here. She'll solve this problem in no time. She'll tell you the truth."

"I'm afraid I can't do that, Raven. For one, we disobeyed their command that day. Second, the two abandoned us, rushing away as we sought guidance to avoid the Exodus." His words told a story pouring regret.

"It's so easy for you to give the command—to kill someone else as if you were the Creator himself," Raven lashed out, "but you aren't. Would you feel the same if your daughter was in my place, dying for a cause she didn't understand?"

"Victoria is always in my mind. She was all those years ago, and she was during the council. My soft heart allowed us to get to this point, but I can't allow it to be soft any longer. If I truly love her, then I must prevent the Exodus from happening."

"What if killing me would bring the end to the Land? Starlight won't let this situation pass by her," Raven replied, trying to convince him of his wrongdoings.

"Don't try to fool me. I know of your true origin. I was there when it all happened. No god of any kind would be incapable of soaring back to the place they come from," Lord Reemus said. He took the candlestick he used to descend the stairs where Raven was imprisoned, preparing to leave. "Rest easy, Raven. Your death shall save the Land. For that, you should be grateful. I won't ask you for forgiveness, I imagine not even Lord Corvix would give me such a thing, but I'll bear the consequences of my actions."

The light of the candlestick flickered for a while before vanishing, leaving the room and the hallway with the usual simple and small candle standing over a table outside. That was truly the only companion Raven had this whole time down in the dungeon.

Raven was alone once again.

They told me it would happen tomorrow just before sunrise. At least I shall see the moon one final time.

The stars remained visible in the sky, but Murdek was nowhere to be seen—at least, not from the small gap in Raven's wooden transport as he was carried across the sky.

After a couple of hours, the sudden thump of the wooden cage hitting the ground made his head collide against the top section of the metal frame surrounding it and announced his arrival to the place where his sentence would be carried out. The sound of trumpets announced something and an apparent crowd went wild, screaming for something. The smell of flowers entered through the gap, carried by a warm summer breeze.

"A very good morning to the Kingdom of the Sparrows," Raven heard Lord Reemus's voice proclaiming. "Thank you all for coming from the furthest parts of the Kingdom to witness this unique moment in Aves' history. I know it's fairly early, and we usually don't work at this time of the day, but I also know you all understand that our duties during the day shall not be disturbed. Therefore, let us finish this as early as possible so the Way of the Aves can continue to guide us away from the Exodus."

The crowd went wild with his proclamation, but Raven couldn't see them. Instead, all he heard was what seemed an uncountable number of Aves surrounding him and a river flowing cloaked by the voices of the masses.

"For years, the Land has been terrorized by a strange ave. Some called it a monster, some called it a stranger, but names matter not, for his acts of violence were felt wherever he passed," Lord Reemus declared to the sound of drums, silencing the population. "Recently, he hailed from the Kingdom of the Owls into our own, unaware that the Sparrows are the most fierce and devoted beings in the Land, and that was his demise."

The drums' beat increased dramatically, preparing the audience's hearts for Lord Reemus's next set of words.

"I give you all… the creature that swore to destroy the Way of the Aves: Raven!"

The wooden walls surrounding Raven's cage fell down in synchronicity with the drum beat, which suddenly stopped as soon as the wood hit the rocky ground, letting the two rivers' confluence be the only sound left.

For the second time in a short period, Raven found himself like an exotic beast left to be gazed upon. Trapped inside his metal cage, he witnessed an enormous crowd of sparrows and other ave caravans surrounding the small island in the center of the Kingdom's capital. Somewhere by the park, near the benches where once Stragif told him he'd met an ave named Eloise—which now he wished had never happened—was a set of thrones. Sitting in the largest one was Lord Reemus. His regal presence could obfuscate the sunlight slowly passing through the enormous trees as the day rose. Right next to him, the piercing gaze of defeat embraced Victoria. She obviously didn't want to be there.

A rock hit Raven's in the face, flying from the crowd, standing in the tree branches and poles connecting the upper layers of the town. So many had come to witness the moment that no empty space for a single other bird could be seen.

"Die, vermin," screamed a voice from the crowd.

"You killed my friend's daughter," yelled another member of the audience, throwing red paint at him. "I hope that is the color we see when you die!" the ave proclaimed. She had the accent of an Owl, most likely a caravan member traveling around or just someone who heard of the event.

The wind carried, once again, the smell of flowers, this time mixed with the scent of salt from the sea hydra.

I did nothing, Raven mentally proclaimed. *I did nothing, and I won't let you all have my life!*

He flapped his wings inside the infuriating small space, his mind attempting to command the will of the wind as he was once taught by his partner. Each time he flapped, he felt his muscles hitting the frames, but it didn't hurt, he had felt worse pains. Yet, they didn't bend, and neither did the wind, for all he could create was a simple blow.

Why can't I control you? How dare you choose when to obey and when to run! You're my wind—mine by birthright! Raven shouted inside himself, commanding the wind to obey.

"Are you gonna show us a display of brutality and monstrosity? Do go on," said the Lord of Flamingos with smugness. Surrounding the plaza were newly installed benches for the Lords to witness the event up close.

Lord Reemus simply made a gesture with his wings, and multiple guards approached Raven, each one carrying a spear, and together, they maneuvered a ball and chain.

They approached him slowly, trying to attach it to him. But Raven wouldn't have it. He pecked each one of them. The talons on his feet attempted to cut them, but the golden armor each one wore protected them. The shaft of a spear hit his face, and his skull vibrated for seconds, time enough for the clanging sound of metal touching metal to be heard—his legs being chained.

The steel frame of the birdcage fell down, and in an impulse, Raven attempted to fly away. He was forced back to the ground, his body hitting it with all the might of a free fall, being pulled down by the iron chains.

The audience laughed at the scene.

You won't have me! Raven shouted to himself, attempting another flight just to meet the same fate as before.

You won't have me! he shouted to himself once more, trying to take flight one more time. But the bricks of the plaza greeted him yet again.

"***You won't have me!***" Raven screamed for all to hear, not only to himself, trying to lift the iron ball from the ground.

But it refused.

Victoria stood up and prepared to rush in his direction, but a gentle hand stopped her.

"Don't do this, your majesty, woo," Stragif said. He himself was chained to the ground.

"I can't watch this, and certainly, you can't, right? He is your friend," Victoria protested.

"Have faith in the Creator, woo," Stragif replied, his voice reminding him of when he had told Phorma and Morpha the stories of the old heroes. "The Land guided us here. The wind aided you to steal the Key. Have faith that none of this happened for nothing."

The laughs of the crowd faded with time, but Raven's desperate cries carried on as the sun rose.

Come, hateful fire, burn my feathers, and give me the strength I need to break free! For once, I'll accept your warm embrace.

But the shade completely covered him, for the plaza at the river's connection was perfectly surrounded by the trees in the early morning.

What trickery of fate is this? Why, Creator? Why do you do this?

The drums resounded once again, and even Raven fell still, listening to the rhythmic patterns. They then came to a halt as Lord Reemus's voice took flight. "The time has come, oh Creator," he proclaimed. "You delivered Raven unto us to ensure the Fourth Law be fully enacted…"

Dexter and George flew from the heavens, downing upon the plaza with a weapon. Each carried a part of a long chain attached to a huge blade, so sharp and thin, Raven almost didn't notice as it descended.

"Only the Creator can give life…" Lord Reemus continued.

His guards approached Raven. This time, no chains were in sight, only the formidable spears. And their shafts didn't point at Raven, for their arrowheads, pointy and glittering things, faced him this time.

"And he is the only one with authority to take it…"

Raven attempted another flight, but it was in vain. The spears flew from the guards, piercing him all over. As he fell to the ground, more pierced through him, carving their head into the ground. He was now bound there.

"The Creator delivered him unto us to enact this law, his will to take life."

The rhythm picked up. Yet, between each successive three beats, a short pause silenced the world.

"There will be no gain in the hands of another's loss."

"Father, stop, I beg you. This is a mistake, can't you see?" Victoria pledged, holding strong to Stragif. "Look at the wounds Dexter's spear delivered him in the cave. They are gone, like a miracle!"

"But you're not one of us, so no loss will be felt, and no gain will be held."

The cold blade still touched Raven's neck, issuing a small cut.

"It's aligned," Dexter said.

"Let's lift it up a little so the fall shall be swift and painless," George spoke.

The scent of flowers carried by the wind's gentle breeze flew past him, adorned by the ocean's sea hydra. His two elements to control were present in abundance, and yet, they ignored him. His eyes gazed skywards, searching for Murdek.

Can you see this, Starlight? Raven wondered. *I'm sorry I didn't listen to you.*

"Let the path to the Exodus…"

Victoria sang her sad tune out of rhythm and order. This time, it wasn't a sign, but her true feelings escaping in song. Little Timus joined from the crowd, and soon, all the hatchlings with whom Victoria had made friends created a sad chorus.

Lord Reemus's announcement came to a full stop. Everyone could see in his face the signs of hesitation. The drums stopped, and one could believe the world stood still; only Victoria's song chanted in that moment, engraving the section of time with music.

"Fly by us and never come back," Lord Reemus finished, giving Dexter and George the signal. Raven closed his eyes.

The blade fell, cutting the air itself.

As the night darkened ever more, the blade changed its direction, flying far towards the river, where it plunged into its depths.

Screams and destruction ensued. The crowd fled the place as panic consumed them.

"Another one?" Lord Grimald proclaimed, his voice shouting, for the sight was unbelievable.

When Raven opened his eyes, he saw George and Dexter each pulling a spear from his body, preparing to attack a huge black bird coming down from the sky, blackening it.

"But they don't look alike," Lord Phoenici proclaimed.

"What is the meaning of this, Lord Reemus?" Lord Saucerottia zapped.

Without a single command issued, Dexter and George knew what to do. They flew in circles around the monster, spears at ready.

With a single movement of its wings, the wind swooped with such strength that the two faithful sparrows lost their formation for a second. But a second was all it needed to break through, passing between them.

"You see, Princess, woo, seems like—" But Stragif was surprised when he saw Victoria picking the lock of the chains around his claws.

"Once this is open, fly the furthest you can from this place," she told him.

"But what about you, woo?"

"Don't worry about me," she finished, letting a single tweet escape. Timus heard it amidst the crazy crowd and took flight with the other hatchlings.

"From the south," Timus shouted, "there is another one coming from the south."

The audience in the southern section of the capitol plaza flew in despair to the north, passing over Raven's location. In their wake, they carried everything.

"We need to leave this place," Lord Grimald said to one of his attendants as his throne was lifted from the ground by a flying sparrow fleeing in despair.

The chain holding Stragif to the Land opened, freeing him from this terrible prison.

"I never thought losing the ability to fly could be so painful, woo."

"No time for philosophy now," Victoria exclaimed. "I need to unlock Raven. Get out of here."

Stragif didn't think twice and joined the crowd where no one would notice him in the middle of such chaos.

Victoria prepared to soar past the tempestuous movement the audience created when she felt wings surrounding her.

"Are you crazy, Victoria?" Lord Reemus shouted. "What do you think they'll do if they see you setting the creature free? They will think your little song was a signal and sentence you to death."

"Better to die here than to live this life of lies you set upon me," she fiercely replied, her voice roaring.

"Once this is over, you'll find a husband and never leave the palace walls ever again," Lord Reemus reprimanded her.

"You'd have to clip my wings. Your chains can't bind me to the ground," she replied with fire in her eyes.

Lord Reemus took flight, carrying her under his wings.

"Father, please, stop," she begged him, dropping her lockpicking tool down into the river.

"Finish the execution!" Reemus exclaimed to every guard around. "Kill them both!"

The monster quickly turned, flying back towards Raven. It went face-to-face against the crowd. In despair, the Aves turned, flying straight toward the ones coming behind them. They hit one another as they tried to find a space to escape from the monster.

And the monster met them, hitting the poor Aves and sending them flying all around. From afar, it could see little sparrow hatchlings removing the spears from Raven's body, but they could do nothing about the chain.

It flew down, grabbing one of the spears left behind.

"Trust me, and don't move," the monster shouted. The creature's blue eyes shone brighter than the sky above them.

Was that a woman's voice? She isn't the same monster from the Kingdom of the Owls, Raven thought, seeing her flight as if the other Aves were not there. Dexter and George, on the other hand, saw only the creature of destruction that they expected. They moved in between the crowd as if they were droplets of rain during a soft shower splashing against a flying ave—they could feel it, but they couldn't move them.

The blue-eyed ave stood in place, flapping her eyes as fast and as fiercely as she could. The sparrows, although strong and powerful, couldn't face the mighty gale pushing them away. Suddenly, they were flung back, falling into the river, whose turbulent hydra carried them away.

Such strength! Who is she? No monster that is for sure, Raven thought as she plunged from the sky. The spearhead was aimed at the chains holding him down, and with a precise hit, they shattered.

"Thank you," exclaimed Raven. "I don't know how to repay this debt." He took flight. The wounds where the spears had pierced him ached, but at this point, pain was like a second part of him, almost a friend that never let go.

"Don't thank me yet. First, we need to get out of this place," the blue-eyed bird replied.

"The ocean, can we get near it without being detected? I have an idea, but I must get there," Raven asked.

"I know a path. Follow me." She led the escape. The remaining crowd opened the way for them, parting in two like a sea. They soared under trees, flying next to the foliage at the crest.

"Maybe we should fly above the forest?" Raven suggested, knowing the sun would meet him there. "I mean, the tree branches are slowing us down, aren't they?"

"If we fly above the trees, all we would achieve would be you catching fire," the mysterious ave replied. "Besides, I'm an expert at running away and remaining undetected. They haven't had the chance to find me before, and they won't have the opportunity to achieve that now."

"I see, you know a lot about me, then," Raven replied, taking note of her comment about his powers. "Our meeting must not have been a coincidence. I'd imagine you know my name, don't you?"

"Yes, I've heard Stragif the Owl say it many times. You're Raven, from Murdek," she replied.

"Yet, I know nothing about you. Can you tell me your name, at least?" Raven politely requested.

"I'm Zola, the monster. I have no idea where I'm from," she said as they both soared in the middle of the deep foliage, seized by the darkness. Raven felt a knowing tug chart his route through the dense greenery. He knew that the Land guided him.

The smell of sea hydra intensified, carrying with it the sound of waves crashing against the beaches that encircled the Kingdom of the Sparrows, slowly overtaking the cries of chaos left behind in the capital.

"Let's turn here," Zola said as the two approached the forest's end.

Raven was graced by the warm ocean breeze and felt, for the first time, free again. It had no taste, shape, or form, but nonetheless, it was a vibrant feeling—a light inside his heart—that made the sunlight pale in comparison.

CHAPTER II

Fugitives

Hydra dropped constantly, each droplet reverberating upon its own demise as it touched the marble rock inside a dark, damp cave. This time, though, the cave was different from the previous ones; the hydra inside was a result of the crashing ocean's wAves entering the cave located right at sea level, just off the coast. It was connected to the Land by a strip of rocks that made the entrance visible for anything that could walk there, and while for the Aves, that wouldn't be a problem, the rising tide would erase the tracks that such a place existed in the first place.

There, Zola guided Raven. The silver Phoenix's feathers shone an incandescent light that almost blinded any that dared to look at him. There was nowhere to hide from the sun past the forest frontier's end as they both glided across the ocean, catching the warm, uplifting winds that easily carried them to their destination.

Zola could see that Raven was in pain throughout the whole flight, putting on a brave face and summoning the strength to live another day. She knew what that meant, to fake something, ignoring that it was even there, pretending it never existed. As far as she knew, for the longest time, she had never existed.

"How are you feeling?" Zola asked Raven after they proceeded further down in the cave.

"I think I will survive," Raven replied, landing on a patch of solid rock halfway submerged under sea hydra. Zola watched as he took a sip of the terrible thing. As she predicted, as soon as she saw the act happening, Raven spit out most of it.

"Why are you doing this? This water is terrible," she asked with genuine curiosity. "Far better were those desert fruits I gave you as you crossed it."

"What? *You* gave us the fruit?" Raven replied in shock.

"Yes, I spent most of the time flying low and moving behind the dunes. I… Well, it doesn't really matter now. You're here and alive," she finished with a certain reluctance.

"Why did you save me? Are you following me for some weird reason?" Raven said. She noticed that his eyes made an analysis of her very slowly. "Are you dangerous like the others of your kind?"

"Oh, please, no, don't confuse me with my brothers. They are not the best kind of people to be around," Zola quickly said. "I've been following you because—" But Raven suddenly collapsed to the ground. "Are you alright?" Zola asked, rushing to his side, the water splashing upwards as she took a quick flight over it.

"I am as good as I could ever be at this point," Raven replied with a certain difficulty. "Those spears did a good number on me, not to mention the sunlight. You've seen it before, haven't you? My body transforming itself into a giant candle…"

"Please, don't talk for now," Zola said. "Rest easy here, and I'll see if there are any ingredients for medicine deep down. I've made it many times to ease my brothers' pain after a hunt."

"There is no need," Raven told her. "I think I have figured out what is so special about this Kingdom that heals me," he added as he tried to take another sip of sea hydra. As with his previous attempt, he spit it all out. "Well, I didn't recall it being that disgusting."

"You've been drinking sea hydra?" Zola asked him back in confusion.

"Eloise— Well, I mean, Victoria brought it to me multiple times to drink, and as I did so, my body grew stronger. A couple weeks later…" Raven said, and Zola noticed that he stopped to think.

Maybe he doesn't know how long it has been. Even I lost track of how long he'd been gone, Zola pondered.

"Well, sometime after that, Dexter— Or was it George? Well, one of those two Sparrow knights that are glued to one another speared me in the back on the path to Mount Kingdom Come," Raven said. "Some sea hydra healed me. I had to hit a waterfall to do it, but I think that was the case."

"Can't you just immerse yourself in the ocean, then? To heal it all?" Zola replied.

"I can certainly bathe in it, but I'm sure I can't dive in," Raven replied.

"So, use this shallow water here. I'll search for medicine, as I told you." Zola prepared to take her leave.

"Wait, I still have so many questions I need to ask you," Raven shouted, attempting to stop her mid-flight.

"Don't you trust me?" Zola coldly replied. "After all I did, the fruits in the desert…"

"No, that isn't it…" Raven was clearly at a loss for words.

"This water might not be safe to just pour into your wounds. Let me treat them first," Zola said, taking flight and proceeding further into the cave.

The creatures inhabiting this cave complex were far different from the creatures Zola used to observe back near her home in the Kingdom of the Owls—not that she had ever considered it her home; in actuality, it was a far cry from one.

Have I ever had a home? A place for myself and my siblings? she found herself thinking, realizing the little white creatures with multiple legs hiding under rocks were beings she had never seen prior. *Raven constantly stares at the moon. Murdek, wasn't it? I need to ask him more about it. Do I have a Murdek of my own?*

Despite how much time Zola spent thinking, every place she'd once called a home was abandoned as fast as she arrived. From lush green peaks to snow-covered summits and, of course, the vivid forest that belonged to the Owls, she had stayed in some lovely places, but they weren't exactly her home. *What is a home? Could it be the place where my parents are?*

Regardless of how far she went, the sea hydra seemed to find a way, creating small links in the system and hallways that seemed to lead deep down, directly to the core of the Land. *Does the Land have a core?* she questioned. *What could exist deep down? Is there a map that shows it?* The questions kept on rolling.

Listen to me. If Zephyr was around, he would say how stupid I am for wondering about unnecessary things. We need to eat and remain together.

Somehow, that final thought held a piece of nostalgia. *He was never a good person, but he cared for us all.*

An immense hollow cavity appeared in front of Zola. Rocky figures all around reminded her of the needles used by the peacocks to thread their fashionable clothes. Some rocks sprouted from the brown floor, piercing upwards. Others hung from the ceiling in different shapes and sizes, creating a jagged territory within which Zola couldn't find a place to land with ease.

After minutes of searching back further inside the large chamber, Zola spotted a green fungi not unlike the one she had learned how to use so many times. Surrounding it, she noticed a vast variety of strange life annexed to the stalagmites, resembling a colorful reef out of water. She broke apart a dried piece that composed the reef, reminding herself that she once heard an owl speak about such things as living creatures, but the piece she took was nothing but a dead rock that once might've lived.

How far does it go? Zola thought, observing that the cave continued far deeper. *When Raven gets better, we can go check together!* she told herself with hope. *Or maybe he'll run away from me like everyone does,* she continued, setting a rock on top of the round, glass feeling she'd called hope a second ago, daring to destroy it herself.

"Ouch!" Raven cried. "This thing hurts a lot!"

"I'm sorry! It might be the salt," Zola told him. "My mixture is usually made with fresh hydra."

"What wouldn't I do for some fresh water right now," Raven told her. "Do you think we're gonna have to live by drinking from this terrible amalgamation that dares to call itself hydra?" Raven continued, insinuating he planned to tell her a joke—one Zola didn't catch.

"I can get us water from the river, but it would be nice if we could get rid of the salt ourselves like the sparrows do," she replied in all seriousness. "I can get out and get the filter they use," she replied, setting the mixture pot she'd created using the reef base on the ground. The water level almost swallowed it.

"Are you leaving?" Raven asked her, turning around in a fast motion.

Zola raised her wings, trying to protect her face from an incoming impact that never came. For a second, she saw a memory of Zephyr hitting her, asking her to never leave. But Raven wasn't Zephyr.

"Are you alright?" Raven asked in confusion.

"Yes, I'm sorry. I just got confused. The smell of salt and…" She tried to wing the situation out, but she stumbled all over it. Every word came out in dissonance with the previous one. Without finishing her sentence, she took flight once again.

"Wait," she heard Raven shouting, "just stay down for a second so we can talk. I still need to know who you are." Each word fell softer in her ears as the distance between them increased and the walls failed to reverberate the sound.

"I'll be back as soon as I get the filter," she shouted back, hoping it would reach him. "I'm sorry."

Maybe if he doesn't ask too much, he won't go away, right?

The sun had yet to set in the Kingdom of the Sparrows. Laying low enough in the sky to create a twilight of red and yellow moving colors, it shifted down towards the horizon as the night sky swept all the colors away as if it was pushing it down a rug.

It wasn't the best of times for Zola to move out and about, soaring and gliding from branch to branch, trying to stick to trees with dense foliage, sneaking her way toward the capital.

"The Dawn of the Dark Feathers will be a day to remember," she heard a sparrow telling another as they flew right under her; a single movement of their heads and her hideout would be spotted. "Let's hope we'll find those two fast."

"Think like that," the other sparrow mentioned. "At least we are not cleaning all the feathers scattered across the plaza."

"I've heard the dark monsters had so many feathers on them that, joined with the audience loss, it made a dam in the river," the other sparrow exclaimed.

"I'm glad I was patrolling the town. I'd hate to be near those monsters." Beyond that, Zola couldn't hear. They had moved too far for their conversation to be anything but mumbling words.

Monster, Zola mumbled in her head, *Raven has yet to call me that. Certainly, soon, he'll notice our differences and see how terrible I am.* The little glass marble of hope hid inside her heart and suffered a small crack caused by the weight of self-doubt that encroached upon it.

She prepared to glide towards another tree when a familiar voice spoke somewhere further in the forest. "I'm glad the sentence failed to be carried out," Zephyr said. "Otherwise, how would I fulfill my vengeance? Not by the wings of another inferior Order."

"It was a pitiful display, I heard," came Zaki's voice, even though she couldn't see him. "Wish we could've watched the stories of his suffering, trying to escape the chains. Oh, how sweet it must have been to see it play out in front of your eyes."

"They talk of another dark monster," Zephyr said. " I sure hope Zola had nothing to do with it."

"Who knows," Zemir's voice added. "Maybe she was trying to save him so you could deliver the final blow?"

"Zola is a vulture-like us," Zephyr declared. "She wouldn't dare to betray us. She knows her place in this world."

A monster: That is my place, brother.

"What do I do with them?" Zola heard for a brief moment coming from Zuri, but her sister quickly fell silent as another patrol came their way.

They are on high alert. I should not stay here any longer, neither for the patrol nor for my siblings.

She flew away, navigating the forest by its outer edges. Next to the desert, lights mounted atop rocks in the distance indicated a caravan resting. Zola hid nearby, watching from the trees the lives of the Aves in the caravan. She quickly noticed this was a special one, though, for it belonged to the dodos—a rare species that couldn't fly and resorted to travel across the Land by walking.

"Hey, mother," she heard a little dodo comment. "Do we really need to walk all the way back? The desert is too hot," he complains.

"Of course, my darling," the mother replied with some giggles. "How would you expect us to return?"

"Well, everyone else can fly. So, why can't we?"

"Everyone is different. The Creator made sure to do that so we could enact the Way of the Aves," she tells him. "We are special in our way."

A group of guard Sparrows approached the caravan. They were quick to surround every member.

"Have any of you seen the fugitives?" one of the guards barked.

"No, sir, we haven't," the mother was quick to answer.

"Hey, mister, why are you hunting them? Why do so many people hate them?" the little dodo asked.

"Because they are monsters. They defy us," the sparrow told him.

That word again, Zola thought, observing the conversation with great interest.

"What is a monster?" the little one followed.

"Well, it is a creature that is different from us. Dangerous beasts that threaten to kill us all," the guard replied.

"But we are different, aren't we, Mom? Are we monsters, too?" the little dodo questioned in deep confusion.

"No," the mother quickly replied. "Remember what happened earlier this morning? Weren't you afraid when every bird took flight in despair and the sky blackened with their feathers? That is what monsters do. They make us feel fear," she told him, almost scorning the little hatchling. "Please, forgive him," she told the guard. "He is still learning the Way of the Aves.

"Don't worry," the sparrow replied. "Little ones don't understand the absurdity of their questions, they just ask away."

The conversation continued for a couple of minutes, but Zola couldn't quite concentrate on it. She'd stayed in hiding for so long; the guards had moved on, and the sun had effectively gone. That was her chance, she swooped into the caravan, and while everyone was reading themselves to sleep, she took a filter from them.

"Mommy, did I upset you today?" Zola heard the little boy asking from inside one of the cars.

"Of course not, my dear. I was just teaching you a lesson when I changed my voice. If there is something you must know more than anything, more than even the Way of the Aves, it is that I love you more than anyone or anything, regardless of anything you do."

Zola's heart stuttered for a moment while listening. *Would my mother love me even if I'm this aberration? Or am I motherless, and that is why I am a monster?*

"Mother," the little hatchling said with a frigid voice, "there is something moving outside. I can see something blue moving."

Zola didn't waste another second. She took flight and soon heard the screams of the dodos, shouting at her, "The monster is here! Somebody, help!"

The cave entrance had almost vanished under the rising tide by the time Zola returned. The guard patrols grew in frequency as the day progressed, and while in the morning, only the Sparrows did their duty, the nightfall brought the personal guard of the other Lords to join the search, knowing the Sparrows had to retire to do their nightly duty—to rest.

"So ironic," Raven told Zola. "They hunted for me the night before, pretending the flame of a torch was the light of the sun itself, justifying their misdeeds. But now that other Lords roam the area, they pretend to do their duty in earnest."

"I learned a word before," Zola said. She took care of Raven's wounds with a proper mixture using filtered sea hydra. "'Hypocrites,' if I'm not mistaken. Or 'ironic,' you say? Well, one of the two."

"You're really smart," Raven told her. His facial expression shifted between fine and agonized every time she touched him with the ointment prepared. "You even knew about the desert fruits."

"I just pick up on things by listening from afar. Other things me and my siblings had to learn as we crossed many places. This desert happened to be one of them. Long ago, we crossed it and almost died of thirst. It was Zephyr, my older brother, who saved us. He figured it out when he stole the fruits from other Aves trying to cross the region."

"I thought the Creator had made the winds to carry those fruits to me and my friend. Now, I see the Creator had no hand on it. Now, I'm left to wonder what else I thought to be divine intervention when the truth seems to take another form."

The sea hydra kept on rising, reaching Zola's wings. To her surprise, the cave's entrance disappeared, and in its place, a deep pond of hydra had surged.

"Can you move?" Zola asked Raven. "The hydra is rising. Maybe we should proceed deeper."

Raven nodded, and the two proceeded further down into the cave. What earlier was a dry system with shallow wet surfaces spread across now was a complex labyrinth of corridors and hallways that found themselves completely submerged. The deeper they followed it, the harder it was to move. In certain sections, they could pass through with only their necks above the hydra level, the cave ceiling threatening to plunge down.

At a certain point, Zola noticed she was back in the long downward corridor—the one leading to the great hollow room where the reef lived. With her guidance, Raven descended, and Zola was quick to notice something different, a light coming at the end of the tunnel.

Sea hydra had flooded the entire hollow area. The stalagmites' flattened surfaces created small inlets of land, like a little archipelago amidst an ocean. That wasn't the most noticeable change, though; it was the reef. The sea hydra touching it brought it life, and a bioluminescent show of colors blossomed from them. They weren't in the darkness anymore but, rather, flying over a rainbow that had grown underwater.

"We can't go any further," Raven noticed. Everything beyond was submerged. "Let's rest on top of the tallest rock," he added, referring to the largest stalagmite that had a flat surface far above the water.

There, the two spent some time, Zola blown away by the show of light. A waterfall was created from the path they took to reach there. The entire cave system was now under hydra; this little empty landing spot they had left was the only place untouched.

"I'm sorry," Zola told Raven, "I brought us to a place that might be our deaths."

"If I'm to die here, at least it's the Land that'll take me, with motes of life coming from life itself, not from a steel, sharp, and cold metal piece used by other Aves," Raven replied.

Zola didn't know how to answer. In actuality, she wanted to fly as distant as she could from Raven. *If I spend too much time with him, he will notice I'm a monster.*

"Why did you save me?" Raven asked her. "That was very brave of you."

"I don't really know. I just felt like that was the right thing to do. I've been following you across the Land, and I saw your struggles, but they didn't. They don't know, they don't care, and they didn't bother to ask. In the end, I felt like they did to you what they always do to me. They run without asking questions, without ever hearing."

"I see, we are very much alike then. Back in the Kingdom of the Owls, the creatures ignored me for the longest time, never bothering to ask how I felt or if I needed help."

"I'm sorry for that. It's my brothers' fault for making people hate us."

"But I'm not one of you. I'm myself. And yet, they failed to see so," Raven said.

"I'm sorry that our actions caused you so much trouble," Zola said as the two grew closer to one another, the water rising ever higher.

"You apologize far too often, you know? There is no need for it," Raven told her. She had heard that before, but the meaning was of mockery rather than of care.

"I'm sorry for being like that," she told him, "and I'm sorry for leading us here to our deaths." The water continued to rise, touching their feet. "I'm sorry," she said again, letting a tear escape.

"Don't say 'I'm sorry.' It's not your fault what they think of us. By showing care for me, you have already demonstrated that you have a better heart than all of them. Now, I finally see it wasn't that the Creator ignored me in the desert, rather, he sent you to save me there and, once again, to save me in the capital. I think I've seen you before, even in the snowstorm, blue eyes flying amidst the two giant Aves. You helped me there, didn't you?"

"I just did what I thought was right, but what does it matter, if it led us here? To the end of our lives?" Zola said, her voice shaking.

As Raven's eyes shined as bright as the colorful reefs, Zola noticed he was having an epiphany.

"No, I now understand something deep that I've seemed to be missing,' Raven said, the hydra reaching their wings.

He embraced her, and for a moment, they were one.

"I'm the God of the Night. The Wind and Hydra are mine to command," Raven said with determination.

The air in the room surrounding them created a circular gust. The hydra took shape around it, and instead of submerging them, it created a pocket of air for them to remain.

"Please, stop crying," Raven told her, the two closer together than Zola had ever been to anything else. "I'll take away all your fears just as you took mine multiple times without knowing. Tonight, I shall protect you."

"I'm sorry," Zola said, not knowing exactly why.

The hydra submerged the entire hollow ground, but it never touched them again, and from such a unique spot, the light of other living beings shone brighter than the sun. But they were not as bright as Zola's heart, for something had awakened in there.

CHAPTER 12

The Story of the Monster

Victoria visited the little hole in the wall that Raven once called a cave. Ever since the Dawn of the Dark Feathers, she kept going there, expecting that he would eventually return there. He never did.

"Let's return," Dexter called.

"We have been here for hardly an hour. We need to, at least, wait a little longer," Victoria protested.

"Your father ordered us to return earlier today," George told her. "He has arranged some potential candidates for you to marry."

I don't want to marry. Not yet, at least. Doesn't he care about my own choices?

Someone glided into the cave, surprising Victoria. The shadow was far too small to be Raven's, so before she could even turn to see who it belonged to, her heart had already sunk for it, most likely, would be a sparrow.

It is my fault. I guided him to the cave where he'd be captured. I have to make amends somehow, she thought, turning around. And there he was, just another guard, carrying a map with him.

"Is this what you requested, Your Highness?" the guard asked, handing her the map.

She opened it over the rock she'd once treated as a table to prepare food. The map charted the entire Kingdom of the Sparrows, the entirety of the desert, and parts of the oceans and peaks surrounding it. Across the entire map, Xs marked a varied set of spots.

"So, those are the cAves and areas we have already investigated?" Victoria questioned the guard.

"It is the most up-to-date we have. It is missing today's location, of course, but it is as you requested," the guard replied.

"Understood, you may go," she told him, sliding the map inside her coat just like she did with the Key in what seemed time immemorial now. "I shall spend the day I have left in my room studying it, trying to see if I can recall anything he said that might help us find him," Victoria felt terrible saying those words. She noticed Dexter was about to say something, so she just interfered. "After, of course, I deal with my father's new attempt at getting me a fiancé," she said, preparing to leave. "Let's take flight, shall we?"

They left the cave behind, no one ever noticing that Victoria's coat had a giant hole in it, and the map was left by itself, on the cave's floor.

It's up to you now, Stragif. You can find him.

The night was almost over when Raven woke up. They continued exploring the cave further, finding a chamber that the water couldn't completely fill, making the place the perfect hiding spot for any that might attempt to enter the cave.

Together, he and Zola transformed the chamber, bringing in pieces of the reef to light up the place. Food could be captured from the ocean and paired with a variety of diet options as the cave system contained a vast fauna, and to top it all off, the filter Zola had obtained managed to get them a nigh-infinite supply of hydra, ready-to-drink. For the first time since the fall, Raven felt like he was actually living freely despite all the walls surrounding him restraining his freedom. In a way, the constant darkness reminded him of Murdek. He even moved to the cave's entrance when the tide was low during the day to see the sun as he did from the hills of Murdek and its oasis.

Raven stared down at the little lake inside what he now called a home. The reefs' brilliant light reminded him of the reflection of the stars in the Kingdom of the Owls,

Despite all the happiness I have here, why do I feel this drive to return home?

Zola approached him, her reflection appearing by his side, close to the stars. His eyes moved towards her, and for a brief moment, Raven caught himself gazing at her the same way Lord Thebas had looked at his wife. Something strange burned inside his heart: a sense of belonging—a sense of discovery. It burned brighter than the pieces of reef Zola repurposed as a necklace, illuminating every time sea hydra splashed on her.

Is that what they meant by having Mount Kingdom Come inside their hearts? In their hatchlings? But if so, what was that physical place the princess guided us to?

"Please, don't go outside during the day," Raven said to Zola, who had just returned from a patrol. "I don't want to live inside this cave alone."

"I don't go far," Zola said. "But we need to know what's happening. The guards are exploring far further than the Kingdom of the Owls, and I'm afraid they are enlisting the aid of other Aves in the hunt. The seagulls might spot us if they dare to follow this deep in the cave."

"No other ave possesses the powers I do. They would die trying to hunt us down here."

"Not if they come in the day or at low tide. It might take longer for them to explore the entire complex, but they will find us eventually," Zola told him, trying to not argue. Raven always thought her voice to be so soft, even when she briefly tried to antagonize him.

"But where on the Land do we go from here? If this cave isn't secure enough, how can any other place be?" Raven questioned her.

"You might go to Mount Kingdom. Come and return to Murdek with her, woo," Raven heard a recognizable voice. The "woo" melted his heart.

"Stragif! You're alive!" Raven shouted, ready to fly and embrace his dear friend, only for Zola to stop him.

"How did you find this place?" Zola asked him.

"By using deduction, of course, woo!" Stragif told her, opening a map. "You see, I just had to figure out which cave would be the most likely place you'd hide Raven, and one with hydra seemed the best choice. I recall you have some powers attuned to it, woo."

"But people must have followed you," Zola continued, "I remember hearing the Council, and I recall that you did *not* help your friend."

"Trust me, woo, the only one that followed someone was me towards you. It's very hard to hide a huge ave such as yourself when flying over the ocean," he calmly said. "It is true that I didn't tell the truth back in the Council, but I had a reason, woo. The Land's very own firmaments would've broken if I did so."

"So, tell us now," Zola told him. "Gain our trust. Explain why Lord Reemus hates different Aves so much despite the fact that neither I, my brothers, nor Raven have ever seen him before."

"That is where you're mistaken, woo. Raven might've never seen him before, but you, Zola, your life is deeply connected to his." Stragif soared down next to the two large Aves. "Do you have some food, woo? This will be a long tale"

Zola let her guard down for a while, preparing for Raven's friend a place to stay. She set up a little bonfire, the skill, as she'd told Raven previously, came from the long nights preparing meals and scaring away the cold so that her siblings could enjoy a nice night of rest.

Stragif's shadow painted the wall of the cave. The scent of salt and other minerals in the air gave the place a mythical feeling, with the hydra dropping from the stalactites echoing in synchronicity with his voice. "Our tale, woo, begins some time ago in the Kingdom of the Crows."

The moon had just dawned over the Kingdom of the Crows, where Lord Corvis, the youngest ruler in his Family of the Crows, had decided to fly eastward, from whence the moon rises. The Kingdom itself was far more developed than others as it remained in the intersection between the smartest of all Aves: the Family of the Crows and the fiercest of them all, the Family of the Gaizer—both parts of the Order of the Corve. Together, in the olden days, before Orders and Families were a thing, they formed a union to survive the Dark Years of Madness. Such actions led to the worst of days for all Aves but themselves—an event only stopped by the Proclamation of the Laws on Mount Kingdom Come.

Lord Corvis continued his path, soaring high above the city, using the smoke escaping from factory chimneys to hide his passage. The capital of the Kingdom of the Crows was unlike any other. The intelligence of the Order managed to make more use of fire than just treating it as a tool to keep the cold away. Instead, they used it as a tool to create movement, allowing easy transportation of objects on large tracks rather than wasting an ave's time having to fly from one place to another. To top it all off, the river's hydra had fallen under their control; a spinning wheel's power created mills that allowed the food to be easily processed and digested.

Despite all these marvelous things, the city displayed intense vegetation, covered by flowers as distant as the eyes could see. That night, Lord Corvis watched from above the twinkling factory flames, and he listened to the sound of the mills grinding food to dust under the eternal summer breeze that blessed those lands. It reminded him of his Order's oath. It wasn't the one from the Law, created to separate Families and Orders, but the one that existed in the heart of each living there, for the nature left by the Creator, was for the Crows to manipulate as they saw fit. In a sense, they believed themselves to be the inheritors of the world.

Soon after, he flew high above the Kingdom of the Gaizers. The elevation of the plateau where they lived was the only thing separating both places. From afar, it was hard to distinguish one capital from another; they both shone in the night with little flaming dots, but while one fire produced steam to manage transportation, the other prepared goods that had been hunted. The Gaizers worked through the night, as the Creator ordained.

Lord Corvis flew over the city and continued his journey eastward, his mind thinking back to his great friend, Lord Reemus, whose daughter, Victoria, had just broken out of her egg. It gave him so much joy to know that his friend had achieved what love can bring forth: the blessing of a new life.

Love. Why does the Creator give us such a thing, just to take it away if deemed wrong? he thought, landing in a place where the moonlight couldn't reach.

"Corvea, my love, are you around?" Lord Corvix called.

A reply came quickly. "Yes, my dear, not only am I here, but I'm ready to do this—to forget this wretched place once and for all," she told him as a madwoman ready to take the actions of a madman. And they both were mad, for that night, they flew away from their Kingdoms without providing a single explanation to those around them.

But no explanation would suffice. The lord of the Family of the Crows running away with the princess from the Family of the Gaizers would bring a rebellion untold, especially as history left a scar in the connection between those Aves in the eyes of all the Land.

Lord Corvis and Princess Corvea lived a life in a secluded paradise, next to one another at all times but never too close. They wanted each other's presence, but they didn't want to break the Fifth Law. They were just happy for the blessed chance to live in paradise together.

But one night, the moon rose far above its normal location, and its light, after countless phases, had come and gone. The seasons had drastically changed the Land that they lived on for many years, and moonlight finally struck the lovers' eyes as they looked deeply at one another. That moment, their souls, their desires, their intent was revealed, and Lord Corvis couldn't control himself, kissing Princess Covea—a sin, the breaking of a vow, and the sweetest moment of his life. Love flowed like a mighty river after a storm, uncontrollable and destructive.

The sun rose the next morning, and to their surprise, five eggs had been laid.

"What have we done?" Lord Corvis asked Corvea, but in truth, he spoke to himself.

"What do we do now? Will we be parents?" Princess Corvea replied with a question of her own, afraid to give a definitive answer.

"Yes," Lord Corvis said with certainty. "We will be parents."

Destiny, however, was a fickle thing, and sins don't go unchecked, for before they could celebrate their new reality, the lovestruck was stupefied as a surprise appeared.

"What have you done, traitor!" Lord Corvax screamed at them after seeing the eggs. "The Creator shall have your head for such a hideous act! Daughter, speak for yourself! When did he kidnap you?"

Their happiness came to a screeching halt. Somehow, after all those years, their families had found them.

"No, Father, I love him. We left together. It was my decision and mine alone," she said, trying to keep the tears away from her eyes. She knew what her act would entail.

"This will be the death of us all," an ave commented, desperately watching over the eggs. "The Creator will kill us."

"Fear not," Emperor Corvideo said, the ruler atop the entire Order of Corve. "Take the eggs and the two as prisoners. We shall call the goddesses to Mount Kingdom. Come and request an audience. They shall guide us."

In the next couple of weeks, the journey across the Land was strenuous, exhausting, and eternal. Lord Corvix felt as if he would die at any moment, almost wishing he could, as he knew their fate had been sealed long ago. Still, he kept his head held high, for his beloved and their children.

During the journey, the Rooks—whose lands were kept under Corve control—joined them across the Land. Next, it was Lord Reemus of the Kingdom of the Sparrows who joined them. He carried the Key and guided the Lords and Emperor of the Order of Corve to the secret cave and beyond, where Mount Kingdom Come awaited them.

After days of flying above what seemed the top of the world, the silence was absolute. Pencil meeting the paper was the only sound heard, coming from the Master Owl, Grenfold from the Kingdom of the Sparrows, while he recorded the events as is the duty of every Owl across the Kingdoms.

They were there, at the peak of all creation, where the Laws were proclaimed, and the gods themselves visited the Land. The clouds were thick and dense that day, blocking the view of anything surrounding it. Rather than a majestic place, the location seemed dry, dead, and inhabited, swallowed by eternal fog.

The two lovers stood next to one another and their eggs, chained at the center of the summit. Surrounding them stood the Rooks army, the guards of the Crows, the knights of the Gaizers, Lord Reemus with the Key, and the Master Owl, Grenfold. Those flocks were the only ones allowed to witness the events their Lords were entangled in.

"Please, great Gods of Birds, people of the JuJuRae and JuJuRana, concede us the boon of your presence among us in this dire hour of need," Lord Reemus called, raising the Key skyward. The sun and the moon, for an instant, seemed to coexist in the same place in the sky, their light shining directly into the triangular object, creating a beacon made of pure day and night.

The void above—holder of the separation between the Land and the space beyond—became inextinguishable light, and through this passage that connected both worlds, two large Aves descended.

The clouds dispersed, revealing a paradise lost. Waterfalls and rainbows flowed in the distance, with rivers filled with life following towards unknown places. Mount Kingdom Come seemed to go on forever. It had to be a miracle that such a place could be kept a secret.

"Who dares to summon the sun and the moon? Hopefully, it shall be good, for it is day, and I'm still asleep," said Starlight. The enormous ashen Phoenix plummeted down from the sky above in a graceful dive, slowing and soaring softly into a pause above the peak. Her halo of life was so majestic that the rainbows in the horizon lost their colors.

"Pardon my sister, her slumber is important for the moon to do its duty rightfully," proclaimed a golden Phoenix. Her feathers embodied the flames of the sun itself, bringing warmth where she moved. "How can we provide assistance?" Sunshine continued proudly. The golden halo around her was so bright that the Aves felt as if the sun descended upon the Land and stood within their reach.

"Forgive us for the sudden call, but we had a breach in the Law," Emperor Corvideo said with empathy in his voice, bowing to the majestic Phoenixes.

"Whatever do you mean?" Sunshine said with authority.

"Your Grace, Lord Corvis, and the Duchess of the Gaizers, Princess Corvea, mated and produced seed," Emperor Corvideo said while attempting to sound as humble as possible. "When I, Emperor Corvideo the Great, assumed my position, I vowed for the Order to be maintained as ordained by the Laws. I now bring the two and their eggs to be judged as birds of different feathers flock together, and I fear the Path of Exodus might open. Accept this a show of good faith—that I love the Creator and intend to make things right."

"Emperor," Sunshine began, "your bravery to speak for your flock and honesty is appreciated, and for that, your life and that of your Order shall be spared by the Creator, for he knew exactly what he did when he chose you. The eggs born from this couple's love shall face their demise by us, and that shall be their punishment, for a parent losing their offspring even before hatching would be punishment enough for them to live in shame for the rest of their days, alone, never to witness each other again, to hear each other again, to be at each other's side."

"I understand the severity of our mistakes," Lord Corvis said, attempting to undo his errors, "but I love her, and she loves me. The

Creator's Second Law states that I should love my neighbor as one loves thyself, and my love for Corvea is larger than what I feel for my own being."

"Silence!" Starlight shouted. "Do you dare to correct your mistakes by using the Creator's Laws as an excuse? Have you not noticed your arrogance? You're meant to love them as you love yourself, not more than your very existence. It's indulgence over a feeling that leads to pure destruction. It was this indulgence over everything that ran the Land dry of food in the Dark Years of Madness, for your kind didn't know how to control themselves beyond their need."

"Please, she is my light in the darkness," Corvis begged. "I can face the death of my unborn children, but I can't face a day without her."

"You can, and you will. Your kind fought nature before. Your mistake shall not be repeated," Starlight proclaimed with severity. "You were granted the title to rule over all Crows, and that is what you shall do for the rest of your days, in pure solitude."

"At least, grant me a final wish, dear goddesses. Grant one final kiss before time and space set us apart forever," Lord Corvis humbly requested.

"I shall give you that final boon," Sunshine said, faster than the obvious denial Starlight would impose.

Corvis took Corvea by his wing, and together, they flew towards the heavens, dancing to the rhythm of their hearts.

"I love you, Vea," Lord Corvis gently whispered in her ears before ushering a final kiss. For all those who witnessed the scene, the silhouettes of the two lovers blessed under Sunshine's beautiful halo with the sun and the moon together side by side created an afterimage in their minds that could never be forgotten. And then, just as the crescendo of their hearts took them higher up in the sky, so they had to come down, each rhythm screaming in agony.

The soldiers surrounded the eggs, arms ready to hand—ready to do the deed and be done with it all. Lord Corvis let the embrace he had over Corvea go and turned his back to her.

"Father, please, help me!" Corvea suddenly shouted as she fell to the ground in tears.

Lord Corvax's heart broke instantly. He witnessed the hatchling he'd once brought into the world lose not only the love of her life but her own children as well.

"You, Grace," Lord Corvax said in despair, "I know that we made a mistake that can't be undone, but as a parent, I can't see my daughter face the loss of the love of her life and her chicklings."

Lord Reemus felt something that instant; the image of little Victoria sprung to mind. That was a feeling he understood far too well.

"The father in me will not allow for this to continue. We are the most powerful of all Aves. We shall raise our own under our laws," Lord Corvax called, raising his wing upwards.

The Lord of the Rooks, the strongest of all Aves, stood ready to fight. With commands from his royal beak, all present stood in attention. "Do you dare to defile the Creator's Law? He made you that way for a reason, and you excuse yourself for not only breaking a vow made to Him but also using the strength he provided against his will," Starlight said, ready to bend the winds and drown everyone with eternal hydra from the sky, for they were hers to command.

"Reason or excuse, I don't care," Lord Corvax said, taking flight, gliding mere feet above the ground, but his presence was imposed above everyone else.

"We haaave to get out of here," the Master Owl, Grenfold, told Lord Reemus. "We will be burned and drown many times over with their kiiind."

"I can't leave. It's a Sparrow's duty to guide travelers in and out of Mount Kingdom Come. We can't leave until we know if their bones shall rest here or they will make sense of the madness they are inflicting upon themselves," Lord Reemus told Master Grenfold.

The wind blew, carrying the tears of a mother; she would leave that place with her hatchlings or see her entire family die.

Lord Corvax let out a war cry so high that everyone present knew it must be heard across all creation. The Rooks charged at the Phoenixes, but Starlight, with a single movement of her wing, undid the wind that gently carried tears, transforming it into a storm that prevented any from flying.

The clouds gathered together, dense, dark, and filled with hydra. Lord Reemus and Master Grenfold were sent far away from the crowd, the wind preventing them from reaching the summit once more.

And then, light everlasting reached the Land from the sky high above. The goddesses looked back at their rightful positions in the sky to find Murdek was on fire; silver flames consumed it.

"The Silver Egg. Has it hatched?" Starlight asked Sunshine.

"If so, we must leave now. The storm carried the eggs away from their grasp, meeting their fatal fate. We can deal with the lovers' punishment later," Sunshine said. "The Creator has blessed us with new life."

The goddesses flew away, returning to the sky, and the sun and the moon split apart, returning to their rightful locations. The storm had ceased.

Lord Reemus and the Master Owl, Grenfold, managed to fly back to the summit. On the way, however, they caught the sounds of treachery happening.

"What do we do with them now?" Lord Corvax said.

"We managed to catch them before they could fall and break," a rook replied.

"We shall keep them, right, Father?" Corvea pleaded. "Right, Father?"

Lord Reemus thought about Victoria and had to make a decision to never ask what happened.

"Lord Reemus never knew the fate of the eggs, woo, for when he returned to get the Key and guide the Crows, Gaizers, and Rooks back, they were nowhere to be seen," Stragif said, finishing his story. "Until very recently, the fate of those five eggs remained a mystery, woo—one that Lord Reemus just happened to stumble upon. The past catches up to him. Do you see, now, why I kept this a secret? Telling every Lord what the Order of Corve did and their defiance against the Creator would lead to a terrible war, even Lord Reemus would be swept in."

"I don't understand. What does that have to do with Raven?" Zola asked.

"Raven, woo? Well, that's just a misunderstanding. It is you, Zola—you and Zephyr and all of your family—that Reemus truly wants. He might feel guilty for allowing you all to be unleashed upon the world."

"Are you telling me my parents are… they are… Lord Corvis and Princess Corvea?" Zola said, her voice shaking. "I was born of a mistake against creation itself?"

Zola's ears waited for an answer coming—something to make her feel better, knowing now she wasn't supposed to exist in this world. It was her eyes meeting Raven's that provided comfort and all the answers she needed. Something burned inside her, and now, she knew what it was. It was the sinful feeling Corvea felt for Corvis. But something that beautiful couldn't be a sin.

"It matters not where you were born," Raven told her. "What matters is that you are my Mount Kingdom Come," he said, embracing her.

"I have an idea, woo," Stragif said. "I think Zola might be our way into Mount Kingdom Come. You see, I believe the eggs never left the mountain with the Order of Corve. Lord Reemus would know of it if they had. So, they might have remained there, woo."

"And how does that help us?" Zola asked.

"Did you perchance use a key to leave Mount Kingdom Come, woo?"

"Well, when we left the place we grew up, we just flew out of it," Zola replied.

"Would you be capable of guiding us back there? You knew your way through the desert, didn't you, woo? You passed by it when you first left," Stragif concluded.

"I might know," Zola said. "I never thought that place held such an important position in history. To me and my brothers, it was nothing but a mountain with vegetation, like the many others where we lived after."

"If you can get us there, woo, then Raven can call upon Starlight and prove his innocence. It'd be the end of it all."

"But what about me?" Zola asked. "Wouldn't Starlight try to kill me?"

"No, I shall speak to her, my dear, and she won't do anything towards you," Raven said. "Please guide us there, and we shall put an end to all this mess, once and for all."

That night, Raven left his hiding place.

Chapter 13

Betrayal

For the first time in a long time, Raven finally saw Murdek flying high up in the sky. That sight, in a different time, would've been able to bring tears to his eyes, but this time, it didn't. No, he felt strangely hardened and used to the distance. Despite the world, the sun itself, and all creation trying to kill him time and time again, soaring over the ocean towards the desert frontier and the place where he was once ambushed, he finally managed to stop and see the beauty surrounding him.

The winds carried him with purpose, the sea hydra rose up and down as he needed, and the light graced his feathers as he glided right atop Murdek's reflection in the ocean. The Land was beautiful when it wasn't trying to kill him.

"How further will we need to go past that cave, woo?" Stragif questioned Zola.

"We shall not fly through the cave, but instead, we shall go above it, far, far above, beyond a chain of unmoving clouds that circles the mountains," Zola replied, her eyes brilliant as if she was reminiscing of the past when she did such a thing, not plotting their future endeavor.

"Interesting that such a thing exists as a set of clouds that never move woo. Unrecorded by any scholar prior, even though it hides in plain sight."

"This, my friend," Raven proclaimed, "shall be yours to record first. I want Mount Kingdom Come to be a place accessible to all, that all shall know how to reach any god at any time."

"Won't we need the Key you mentioned in your tale?" Zola asked Stragif. "Lord Reemus used it to summon the goddesses, didn't he?"

"In general, Zola, I don't think so, woo. When the goddesses first visited our world, such an object didn't exist, and yet, they came nonetheless. But I prepared for such an inconvenience, and that is why we must stop at the Frontier, where Victoria shall join us with the Key."

"Such a brave woman that one is, an ave like no other, defying her father time and time again," Raven said.

"I think it'd be better if we didn't have to face our parents at all," Zola said.

"My daughters defy me just as often as they obey me, woo, and yet, I'm certain they love me. It is part of growing up for one to find their place in the world by surpassing their elders and doing the unimaginable," Stragif said.

Despite the fact that Raven had barely spoken with Stragif's daughters, Raven had a kind view towards them as the moment he'd first laid his eyes on the two little ones had been the moment Raven had finally gained Stragif's trust, and trust was something lacking in the Land. From Lord Corvis and Lady Corvea, who betrayed their kind for love, to Lord Corvax and the Rooks emerging as enemies of the Creator himself or Zola's brothers who, for as much as they cared for her, also set her apart, not to mention Victoria or Eloise; in that case, the embodiment of misguidance, trust was an article in dire need to be rebuilt.

Mount Kingdom Come reopening to all shall connect the Land with gods such as myself. We shall unite together, he thought to himself, but there was something deeper in that thought—a feeling he began to suppress the moment he embraced Zola in the cAves. He hid it away, deep at the bottom of his heart and mind, covered by a warm blanket formed by a strange feeling, relatable to him as the feeling Lord Corvis felt for Corvea. At least, of that, he was sure.

Is this Love? he asked himself, watching Zola be bathed in the moonlight. *How would Starlight react to this? I was to be her partner, but I don't want to do so anymore. What would Sunshine say? For I am a Phoenix—a JuJuRae born to rule the night—and she is a being that calls herself a vulture—birds of a different flock. I'm the purest being that there is, heavenly is my conception, and she is the result of sin. Sunshine would never approve.*

"What bothers you so much, Raven, woo?" Stragif asked, taking Raven out of the jail of his mind.

"Just the cruelty of it all. The tale woven by the Creator knows no boundary for beauty, but in equal measure, it delivers sadness," Raven replied.

"Listen, woo," Stragif whispered, flying next to Raven. "This might be a trick used by her to convince you. Those 'vultures,' as they call themselves, are evil beings born of unlawful act, woo. Have you forgotten what they did to my children?"

"She isn't like her brother, or any of her siblings, for that matter. Zola is special, kind, curious, unique, and… She is Zola," Raven said. A long sigh escaped after the final words. Her name carried power in his mind.

"Birds of a feather flock together, do they not, woo? She might not know yet, but intent runs deep in one's blood. The Sparrows wouldn't abandon their duty, not even when called 'Eloise.' Victoria only managed to persevere because she felt it was her duty to protect Mount Kingdom. Come and aid the Gods of Birds, woo," Stragif denounced.

"You're just hurt and mistrustful of her, and for good reason, my friend. Your daughters and wife almost met their deadly end at the hands of her family. But you'll notice, as did I, how important it is to trust others. It lights your heart out of the darkest pits and creates the wind that will carry it out to freedom," Raven told him.

"If later this act beaks you in the back, woo, you won't need me to say, 'I told you so.' After all, I'll be there to carry you out of the darkness as you did for my soul on that horrible night."

When the trio arrived back at the cave in the Triple Frontier, the moon had passed well above their heads, announcing that half of the night had come and gone.

"Victoria should be waiting for us with the Key, woo, deeper in the cave but not as far as I went last time."

"Choosing this place is almost like laughing in our faces," Raven pointed out. "Why would she return here?"

"Why would they look for you in the dark, damp cave that you once were defeated in?" Zola argued, trying to understand Victoria's reasoning.

"Oh, that makes sense." Raven didn't really know that it did, but he wanted to let a compliment appear somewhere, and there is never a better time to do something than the present. It was strange how the last couple of days had given him so much insight into the passage of time and the worth of every second. Experience and terror were the best teachers to prevent mistakes, he believed.

The group went in, following the ruins left by birds of ancient times.

"Why do you think those exist?" Zola asked Stragif, pointing out at the pillars of yellow and brown stone rising from the floor. They towered over the bottomless cave and were a strange visage in the dark, silent as they stood between waterfalls that never ceased to scream about their presence, the scent of salt corroding the air.

"There are no records of it, woo," Stragif said, guiding the group as he was the only one who could perfectly see in the dark. "Master Owl Grenfold told me, during my imprisonment, a little about it. They date back to even before the Dark Years of Madness. It is likely that, during the ages of abundance, this passage was used by the Aves, those pillars showing how much they could take of the Land without giving anything back. Another idea is that Mount Kingdom Come was a place of adoration even before the Proclamation of the Laws, woo," Stragif added in a dense tone. The Dark Years of Madness were seen as a terrible time, but the years leading to it also fell under horrific criticism.

"So many interesting mysteries might be hidden around the world," Zola said. "I'd love to see more of them—explore more."

"What about Murdek?" Raven asked her. "Would you like to come to Murdek with me?" His heart skipped a beat in anticipation of the answer. He only then thought of the possibility that she might not be able to visit the moon, or worse, she might not want to visit the moon.

"Of course, I would. It is an entire new world, like the Land itself! And I would have you as a guide, right? Right by my side, right? Oh, I am sorry. I shouldn't take the time of a god."

"It'd be no problem," Raven replied, his heart lifted out of the burden of not knowing. "Did you notice something just now?" he continued, asking Zola.

"Did I do something wrong?" Zola replied back, clearly at a loss for his meaning.

"You see, you did it again!"

"What did I do? I don't follow you. Is it my wings? Are they flapping wrong? The air here is terrible, I must admit," Zola said.

"In this darkness, I can hardly see your shape beyond your blue eyes, so that is a no," Raven seemed to joke.

"Oh, that was a good guess, though, don't you think? I know you can feel the wind like any ave, maybe even better than most!" Zola said with a laugh. "So tell me, what am I doing wrong?"

"It is not that you're doing something wrong. In fact, you're not doing anything at all," Raven told her. "For the past few days, you kept the term 'I am sorry' away from you. And I'm glad to see it. No one should apologize for just being."

"Oh, I am sorry for not noticing," she said with a quick laugh.

"We are close, woo," Stragif said, lifting his wing. "I can feel someone is nearby."

A couple of eyes opened in the darkness. The yellow and red colors of death told the truth about their intentions even before a single word was spoken.

"Zephyr, is that you?" Zola asked in confusion.

"Thank you for guiding them here, my dear. Family is everything, after all," Zephyr said, his maniacal and deep voice controlling the darkness in the cave, almost as if the hollow space they were in belonged to him.

No, this can't be happening. She didn't do this. Why, Zola? Why? Something is out of place here.

Another four sets of eyes opened, revealing an entire group hiding in the blackness.

"It is high time for a family reunion," Zephyr said.

"Zola, what is happening?" Raven asked her, his mind brewing with conspiracies.

"I don't know. I— I'm sorry, I just don't know. But I don't have anything to do with it," Zola cried in despair, a beg shouted in the void to be heard and trusted, with no other voice ever reaching her. "Raven, please, you have to believe me…"

"You know what disgusts me about you, Raven? It's the fact that those stupid Sparrows dared to think you belonged in my family—that we were equal—but we are not. No, we aren't. You are a monster of the highest order," Zephyr said. He closed his eyes and began to move, the song of his immense wings moving the air in a way that would announce his location in another situation, but not here, where the walls returned every noise from every direction.

"I agree that we are not the same and that the mistake they made was horrendous. But I'm no monster, not even close. I don't kill, and I do my best to do no harm. It is the Land's inhabitants that, time and time again, acted against me, forcing my wings against their might. But you, Zephyr… You chose every victim you had."

"Zola, don't worry about it, just come to our side," a disembodied female voice said from somewhere in the chamber. Their eyes had been closed, allowing them to disappear into the void.

"Zuri, please, we can talk over it. This situation is not in your nature. You can escape it, too!" Zola spoke, though her voice still failed at points.

"Why are you like that, Zola?" a masculine voice began, "Zuri understands the purpose she plays. Everyone has a role in a family. Isn't that what Orders and duties are for?" His voice told of an ave who delighted in his own tone.

"Zaki, we are not born with an Order or duty chosen by the Creator. Let Stragif the Owl tell you. He will explain it all. We are… We are… monsters…" Her voice slowly lost its sound, shrinking into a whisper before vanishing. With each passing word came understanding, a realization slowly forming in her head. "I think—"

A strong clashing sound vibrated across the cave. It was simple, not made of spears, not made of falling debris, breaking rocks, or just the waterfall carrying something from the ocean that fuels it. No, it was the sound of flesh meeting flesh and feathers greeting one another. It was a slap, simple and yet effective for the purpose it was chosen.

Zephyr opened his eyes. He was double the size of Zola. She disappeared in front of him. Her eyes were closed. She was crying.

"You think too much, Zola. Just stop and listen, for once," Zephyr said, surprisingly calm, his wing resting at her face, but Raven couldn't properly see it.

"I'm sorry, brother. I just thought that… I'm sorry…" Zola whispered, almost to herself, but all could hear, for no sound could go unnoticed in this place once you knew where to focus your ears.

I'm sorry, Raven thought as his heart sank. Those were words he didn't want to hear, but still, he did, focusing on Zola the most. *My heart tells me she means every word she speaks. I feel this urge that… I feel this need. I won't let her apologize for things she didn't do anymore!*

The wind picked up inside the cave, centralizing around Raven.

"Zemir, I thought you said he can't use his powers when the moonlight isn't touching him," Zephyr shouted, the turbulence of the wind muffling his voice.

"That was my hypothesis. I don't know how his powers work!"

Raven could not see the two, but the wind told him of their location, as he could feel each flap of a wing aimed to keep them airborne.

"Raven, stop. You don't need to do this," Stragif said, the "woo" vanishing again as he grabbed Raven by the wing. "I beg of you, don't use your powers here."

But Raven didn't listen. His mind was locked somewhere else. The flows of hydra revealed themselves to him just as they had back in the Kingdom of the Mountain Eagles. Raven could see them all as an afterimage, flowing not only above, in the falls but also beyond the walls. The sturdy ceiling was now shining in blue, for he discovered that the entire top section of the cave contained a secret lake formed by the sea hydra.

"Take your wings off of her, or I'll kill you, Zephyr," Raven told him. The wind was out of control.

"Killing by choice, then? The hypocrisy!" Zephyr shouted, bursting into a maniacal laugh as he held Zola ever closer.

Raven felt something strange, the presence of others in the cave. From the entrance, he could feel an army approaching, but further down, from the direction the vultures waited for them, three creatures waited. One was far smaller than the others.

What is going on here?

But before Raven could properly think, Stragif tackled him—a movement so surprising Raven couldn't even use the wind to notice it coming.

The wind current stopped, and in the dark, Raven heard Zephyr flying away with Zola. She tried to shout back ask for help, but she couldn't. Raven ignored Stragif's actions and tried to bend the wind again.

"Stop! You're gonna kill my family," Stragif shouted at Raven with all his strength. But Raven didn't listen. Zephyr, Zola, and everyone in the cave were engulfed by a tornado. The storm's eye was fixed on Raven, but they were all being pulled towards it.

Raven burst into flames. The mighty colors of the rainbow flickered inside the blaze. A strong power emanated from him. The light revealed all under its beautiful hues. The vulture family was there.

Stragif was there. Morpha, Phorma, and Stragif's wife, Griphi, were there. The army of the Sparrows was there.

Zola allowed herself to ride the wind current and to be flung to the center of the vortex. She embraced Raven, allowing the flames to burn her feathers. But not for long. Raven came back to his senses as he felt her embrace and the pain she was feeling.

"I'm sorry," Zola said as the entire cave returned to its original owner—the eternal, hollow void.

"Morpha, Phorma, my love, where are you?" Raven could hear Stragif shouting in the middle of nowhere. But he didn't care.

"I'm sorry, but it's my duty," Raven heard Zuri saying as Stragif's children screamed. But he didn't care.

"We had a deal, owl. You were to bring him and suppress him. Your family is mine to take," Zephyr said in a fit of rage. But Raven didn't care.

"I *did* bring him here. You are the stupid one that made him turn. Give my family back!" Stragif shouted. But Raven didn't care.

"In this sacred place, all shall end," came Geoge's voice, his spears flying next to him.

Stragif flew towards the sparrows. A flash of light illuminated the cave, just like when they were ambushed an eternity ago. The full army of the Sparrows stood there, shaking and out of formation, but there they were still.

"Save my family, please," Stragif begged George. His eyes closed, knowing that last time, they had burned for days.

"You did your duty by arranging this meeting. We shall save your family," George told him. "Soldiers, prepare. The Owls are to be kept safe. Everyone else must die."

"Wait," Stragif said. "That wasn't the bargain. What about Raven?"

The sparrows took flight, spears at wings, marching towards the vulture family. Standing in time, the two love couples were frozen in perfect harmony. The sparrows passed them, rushing with a war cry. But Raven didn't care.

"I'm sorry," Zola finally said again. "I wish we had stayed back at the cave."

A spear plunged through Zola's wings, her blood spitting all over Raven. Dexter was holding it.

This time, Raven cared.

Chapter 14

The Beginning of the End

Zola's body fell from high above, motionless. The light from the contraptions of flames brought by the Sparrows paled in comparison with the Silver Phoenix's rainbow flames, painting the cave in different shades. So strong it was, the entirety of the place revealed itself; the walls, waterfalls, and pillars became visible as far as the eye could see.

The wind grew out of control. Soldiers flew left and right, colliding against one another. Their spears pierced their own friends. Unanimously, the present Aves made a decision without talking to one another, allowing themselves to be carried downwards slowly, losing lift so that the wind would lose reign over them. Their feet touched the base of what Raven had once thought to be a bottomless pit cave, finding deep, purple vegetation, wet surfaces—some covered in the ever-flowing sea hydra—and structures not unlike nests and resting poles, established in a time-long gone.

Above all of them, a silver sun was shining. From its core, one could see every possible color, but all that reached out into the distance was a faint glow similar to the moonlight's silver.

My friend betrayed me, bringing all of my foes to kill me, Raven thought. *My partner abandoned me, never leaving the sky to search for my location,* burned in his mind.

The sun scorched me every day. Why would the Creator do that? he thought in pain. *The Aves hushed their thoughts, killing me and others without first asking, listening, thinking...* The pain grew, slowly transforming itself through ire and rage.

And now, this cruel joke tries to take away the star in my sky, the only person who apologized before anything has even been done or said... His hate grew ever stronger. *I'll accept this power, whatever it is, and I'll burn the Land down. This isn't a sacred place. It is an abomination that requires taming.*

Stragif landed somewhere unrecognizable. The sad sun burning above him was the only thing he could see. He dared not to open his eyes to their fullest, afraid they might burn. But the little he could see reminded him of something.

He shines just like during the moment of his fall. This isn't purely Raven's powers as the God of the Night. This goes beyond such capacity. This might be related to the star.

"Stragif, sir," George called to him, spear at hand, "we landed together. Is there a way to stop this?"

"General George, please tell me you know of my daughters' location," Stragif begged him, trying to approach the proud sparrow, but the wind made even walking difficult, and he had this strange feeling that the hydra beneath their feet was moving of its own, nontidal accord.

"I do not, sir. Everyone has been scattered by the winds in all directions. This place is not only deep and large but also vastly unexplored. We must make haste if we want to find them." George tried to lift himself from the ground, and the wind took him for a brief moment, attempting to drag him up toward Raven's uncontrolled rage.

"It seems like we are walking," Stragif told George. And walk they did. The ruined structures and the corpses of Sparrow knights pierced by their own weapons lay around, giving them the feeling of being in a war—something most of them never even heard about beyond those from families inside the Order of the Rooster. This sadness was only worsened by the cries and random movements of Raven in the fake sky above them, raging out, left and right, like a rabid creature.

"How do you suppose we deal with that?" George asked.

"I can't really tell you. This is something no book ever prepared me for," Stragif said, but he quickly noticed that it was a lie, recalling Morpha's contribution to his notebook. The first page had shown a drawing that inspired Stragif to take up this journey: an image calling him the Rainbow Hunter.

It is time for me to become that. I'll figure out a way to save the Land, I fear Raven might now be threatening.

"Something on your mind?" George asked, noticing Stragif had dove inside himself.

"I was just wondering about my duty as a parent," Stragif said. "I seem to understand far better now about how painful it must have been for Lord Reemus to take the path he chose—to deal with the consequences of his actions the way he did."

"You did nothing wrong. Creatures that didn't belong to the Land threatened us all. They kidnapped your family," George told him. "Making the choice to take them all out of this situation is a rightful duty you carried—one not of the owl but of a father. We knights also carry our own values beyond what it simply means to be a sparrow. That Stragif, sir, is a duty created even before every Order and Family had been organized in the pure world of the Creator," George finished, his hands touching the piled rubble of an ancient era.

"I never took you for a philosopher," Stragif told him, attempting to keep his mind as far as possible from the madness that had befallen them.

"I was present for every lecture Princess Victoria took under Master Owl Grenfold's tutelage. Perhaps some of it rubbed off on me."

"Perhaps..." Stragif said as they continued to walk for what seemed like an eternity, the environment fighting against them.

"What lucky strings of feathers I must have," came a menacing tone. Zephyr was smiling as usual despite the horrid situation he found himself in.

Zola awoke incapable of moving. One of her wings shifted with difficulty. Her last memories were of pure pleasure followed by pain in a long fall, seemingly endless. Somehow, though, she'd survived.

The scenery was quite different from what she remembered: Red flowers with purple leAves were scattered across the whole region, covering the walls and pillars from a different time. The sky screamed in agony, and the sun moved in disarray, emitting all the spectrum of colors that slowly refracted themselves towards a faint silver light. Such a view gave her the impression that the night had come, but the day had never left. She was trapped in a twilight that didn't display orange colors; the closest thing to that tone was the red blood pouring out from her left wing.

What is happening? Is that you, Raven?

Zola tried to call for him, but a screech came out rather than words. She was so tired of it all—the hunting, the chase, the monsters in the dark. The waterfall created multiple ponds and river flows, one of which Zola used to wash her wounds.

She screamed, briefly and softly, but a scream nonetheless. *I wish I could heal this just as fast as Raven does.*

She saw a reflection in the water. Her face had markings on her cheek where Zephyr had given her a slap. Only her injuries and the reef necklace she'd been wearing were distinct features, but beyond that, it was the same Zola she had always seen.

I'm stupid to believe that I could change. This necklace is nothing more than an attempt to hide my older self—to believe in the new—but this bruise on my face shows me who I really am, she thought to herself, almost ripping the necklace apart. But she lacked the strength to do it. Something deep inside her told her not to. It was a voice she couldn't hear as whatever this was, it didn't speak a single word. But she could still feel it, calling her and telling her to go on.

The voice inside herself grew stronger. She felt as if this feeling doubled in size every time she heard Raven screaming in despair. She wanted to scream back—to call to him and calm him.

She would need a higher place if she wanted her low voice to reach him, and so, she began her travels across this forgotten place in time. The flow of the river brought her more bodies than she could count. She claimed a spear from one, and her mind was called back to a recent scene—one in which she rescued someone important to her using a spear to shatter his chains. This memory brought her the strength she needed to carry on.

Far in the distance, she could see a broken down pillar—one that she might be able to climb if only she kept walking towards it.

"Get away from me," she heard a child scream amongst the vegetation.

"Father, help me!"

Zola rushed towards it. She knew those had to be Stragif's daughters. After passing through dense foliage, she arrived at a large, decrypted old nest, enormous and full of entrances and exits. The ceiling had crumbled down, leaving a large entrance both on top and underneath it. Zola spotted, for a brief moment, a familiar complexion and ushered her name without delay.

"Zuri. Whatever you're doing, sister, you don't need to."

"Zola, why do you treat me so? You abandoned us," Zuri shouted from afar with Morpha under her wing. "You have no right to be around when you don't care about your family. Or maybe it's the family of others now that you find yourself enamored by," Zuri claimed, pulling Morpha closer to her.

"I know you don't want to do this. I know Zephyr treats you as bad as he does me. But you can leave. You can find something different in a different place," Zola told her.

"Do you think everyone is like you? Capable, brave, ushering themselves into danger for others? I can't do anything. Every ave in sight would destroy me, break me apart," Zuri cried.

"They do that to me, sister, but I can tell you, some are different. The princess is different. Didn't you used to like the tales of royalty, using them to put yourself to sleep after Zephyr mistreated you? They are real. Victoria is just as great."

"But I'm not a princess unless I'm the Princess of the Monsters," Zuri bitterly said.

A spear plunged from the sky, hitting Zuri in the tail. A clump of her black feathers was lost, but no damage was sustained. From the sky, Dexter rode the wind as if the storm wasn't there, plunging down at high speed to recover his weapon.

Him, again. I'm tired of this guy.

Zola rushed across the pond towards him just as Zuri ran inside the crumbling nest, leaving the spear behind.

"You won't touch my sister," Zola called, trying to get his attention.

"Excellent, I can keep the bargain with the owl, save a hatchling, and kill two monsters in a single place," Dexter said, readying his spear to fight Zola.

The spear flew. The wavering air made it difficult to pick up speed and plummet to the ground before it could reach Zola. She decided she couldn't keep Dexter nearby and ran back inside the dense vegetation, expecting Dexter would follow. That he did.

Dexter soared with ease. He grabbed the spear as he made the wind his own. For Zola, that would be impossible, her left wing was far too gone. Instead, she hid herself in the middle of bushes, spear ready to attack but hoping she wouldn't need it.

Droplets of sea hydra fell from the ceiling, carried by the wind. They came in contact with the reef of her necklace, and the bioluminescence triggered. In an instant, she felt something coming from far above. She looked up just to see a spearhead plummeting from above, Dexter holding it steady to prevent the wall of wind from acting in Zola's favor.

She blocked the incoming attack with a spear of her own and pushed him backward. The wind picked up. Dexter's spear leaned, and he lost his balance, allowing Zola to run away as he was conveyed by the wind to another place.

I can't remain where the water can reach me, Zola thought to herself, rushing away from the vegetation and towards the old nest structure Zuri had gone to. Her necklace acted as a beacon for all to see.

George didn't waste any time and attacked Zephyr. The vulture tried to take flight, but his large body acted against him, pushing him downwards.

"Where are my daughters?" Stragif called. "Where is my family!" Raven seemed to be acting in accordance, for he also screamed in the sky. The light was getting brighter.

"I hope they are all dead," Zephyr told him, "each one of them." He pushed George away with his enormous wing, larger than the Sparrow knight's entire frame. But George didn't give up, aiming the spear to pass right across Zephyr's skull. He grabbed it with his beak.

"Huh? Is that all you can do?" Zephyr said. A smirk showed, even while his beak kept the spear firmly latched. "***Fly, little creature. Fly into the wall!***"

He flung George upwards using the spear as a lever. As George was swept higher into the sky, he opened his wings in an attempt to assume control of his flight, only to find himself being carried even further away from Stragif and Zephyr.

From there, Stragif witnessed the sparrow make a call; from high above the ground, George sang a brief song. He clenched himself, his body assuming a different shape, trying to imitate a rock. George aimed his beak downwards and allowed gravity to be his master, controlling his descent while he maneuvered with small increments to adjust to the ever-changing wind.

The view was spectacular. The remainder of the Sparrow army took flight, allowing the current to carry them all around, waiting for the moment they touched the place where George had been when he did the call, clenching their bodies and allowing free fall to take them.

One by one, they reached the ground, surrounding Zephyr.

"Reveal where the family is, monster," George said.

"Or else you will kill me, correct?" Zephyr replied with a smug grin. The spear he held in his beak looked like a toothpick to him. "You will kill me regardless, won't you? That is what you do. A knight only lives to kill."

"A knight lives to protect. Don't distort our duty to fit your view of the Land," George commanded.

"So, you understand why I kill, don't you? To protect my family. That is *my* duty," Zephyr replied. Stragif noticed a hint of sarcasm in his tone, but that was most likely just the way Zephyr delivered his thoughts. As with every action he took, his speech came in a twisted way. He'd torture his sister, believing that would keep her safe; he'd believe himself honorable in his killing, just like a knight, all the while mocking one.

"Prepare your weapons," George shouted for the dozen sparrows that reached him. "This one is beyond saving."

The army prepared their weapons—the half a dozen that had one; the remainder stood ready for anything. All strode in a circle around Zephyr.

The trees were flung from the ground. The visage was one Stragif had once seen, back in the Kingdom of the Owls, when Raven was under chase against Zephyr. The guards broke formation, evading the projectile, just to find themselves under attack by another flying tree.

Two vultures arrived and joined Zephyr's side.

"You're alright, brother?" Zaki asked.

"You didn't need to scream that loud, you know?" Zemir said. "Now, everyone truly knows your location."

"Let them know," Zephyr said. "Let this place be their grave as we kill them one by one."

"Fly, little creature. Fly into the wall!" Zola heard Zephyr shout in the distance, revealing that he wasn't too far from the crumbled nest in which she was desperately rushing around to search for her sister.

Zola moved between walled-off sections with great difficulty. Most of the interior was built under the assumption its user would be capable of flight, something Zola wasn't just then. She pushed her way through, climbing the steep walls using her claws and the spear as climbing tools, piercing the fungi-covered yellow stone. The passes had been overgrown with vegetation. Some sections of water had poured in, and the high salt content pouring in from the sea hydra waterfalls had damaged most of the structure. Despite Zola's desperate chase for her sister and Morpha, she couldn't stop her mind from wondering what great ave used to live in here and where they had gone. *Could they still be around, with a different way of living?* she thought. *Maybe, after this is all said and done, I'll ask Raven to search for it.*

Raven...

An overgrown type of strange tree moved like it was alive. The foliage couldn't stop in one direction.

"Let me go, you dumb ave," she heard the voice of an innocent girl demanding freedom behind the dense, purple foliage.

Zola readied her spear. Her thoughts were moving so fast inside her head, filling her with doubts. *I don't want to hurt you, Zuri. Please, don't make me do it.*

The foliage shook more and more, the fallen leaves trailing upwards, joining the disjointed wind. Something was coming out of it, and when it did, it was tiny—so small the wind almost dragged it up with the fallen leaves.

"Ahhh!! Another one!" Morpha screamed when she noticed Zola.

"No, I'm here to help you," Zola cried, running towards her.

"The monster wants to spear me," Morpha shouted as she recoiled, ready to run back behind the trees she came from after noticing Zola had a spear pointed at her.

"No, this is a misunderstanding. I'm no monster," Zola quickly replied, loosening her grip on the spear shaft, allowing the head to point away from Morpha.

Like a shark on the hunt, Zuri jumped out of the trees and grabbed Morpha once again.

"You see, Zola, they all call us monsters, even a little one. Why do you deny that?" Zuri questioned her sister. Somehow, Zola noticed a sadness in her question.

"She just doesn't know any better. Her elders taught her to fear the unknown, and we are the unknown right now," Zola said. "How can you expect anyone to like us when all we do is hurt? We hurt even ourselves," Zola added, her wing passing over the place Zephyr had slapped her. "Please, sister, listen to me…" Zola took slow and light steps, approaching Zuri in the safest way possible.

A tweet from afar echoed across the cave, catching Zola's attention.

"I need to go," Zuri said. "Zephyr seems to be in trouble, and he is not too far."

A shadow passed over their heads, flying the winds. *Him, again?* Zola thought, getting ready for another confrontation with Dexter, but instead, she saw a different sparrow riding the wind. And then, she saw another and another.

What are they doing? Where could they be going? she thought, but something else caught her attention: Zuri, who watched the same scene playing out, her mind distant as she was most likely trying to understand the Sparrows' plot.

Zola didn't think twice and rushed her sister, their bodies slamming against one another. Her left wing tackled against Zuri's right, and the wound opened up, but she ignored it, keeping her sister under restraint.

"Run, little owl! Get away from here," Zola cried.

Morpha followed her instructions, but instead of running, she attempted to fly. By virtue of her body being too small, she was caught in the upward stream, lifting her from the ground and stripping her of any control over her movements.

"Ahhh! Help me! Someone, help me," Morpha cried. The whims of the wind moved her left and right without any sense of purpose. Zola let go of her sister and took flight, allowing herself to be carried away. Her left wing couldn't flap, so she hoped luck would be on her side, and the streams would carry her upward.

In a matter of seconds, Zola was within reach of Morpha, grabbing her.

"Are you alright?" Zola asked. "I hope you aren't hurt." She expected an answer from Morpha, but the girl froze there in silence, crying without making a sound.

"I'm sorry," Zola said. "Everything I do always makes others feel terrible."

Closing her wings and using her weight, Zola allowed herself to be carried down, looking for wind gusts not as strong as the ones closest to Raven.

"No, that is not it," Morpha finally said. "I'm crying because I let my parents down once again. My mother told me to not call other Aves monsters, and I did it to you. But you… But you… still helped me…" the little one continued, crying between the sentences.

"It's alright, everyone makes mistakes—"

Dexter approached Zuri underneath them. Zola's sister was still on the ground after her attack.

"Get away from her," Zola screamed, plunging from above, adhering to a similar shape taken by the sparrows she'd witnessed moments ago. "***Get away from her!***"

Dexter dodged her as if he was dancing. Zola, on the other hand, missed her target and made a desperate stop, but under the speed she was falling, all she could do was redirect her speed and hit a wall while keeping Morpha protected. The world went dark for a couple of seconds, but Zola didn't know if it was her failing consciousness or Raven causing the change.

Dexter spared no time. He soared towards Morpha and captured her.

"Let me go! You're so strange," Morpha told him.

"We have a deal with your father. I shall reunite you with the rest of your family," Dexter told her.

The sound of a wall breaking in the distance caught Zola's attention. It was Zuri, running away towards Zephyr's voice.

The girl is in good hands. I need to protect my family, Zola thought, running after her sister. *Creator, how I wish I could fly! These feet are far too slow,* Zola sadly thought as her left-wing ached beyond imagination.

She noticed, as Dexter took flight carrying Morpha with him, that he ignored her completely.

"***Get away from her!***" Raven heard somewhere in the distance, but his mind didn't allow him to look towards it. The voice soothed his heart for a second, and at that moment, the flames vanished.

The cave returned to darkness, but Raven wasn't truly there; he was inside a different dark space—the one his mind created to trap him and show him his true feelings.

Starlight abandoned me down here, his mind told him. He felt as if that voice wasn't a part of himself. The flames reignited once more.

The Creator made a sun that hurts me, his mind reminded him. The pain of the desert passage reignited as a phantom.

My friend sold me for his vengeance. His mind showed him an image of Stragif's eyes staring at him as he spent his days alone by the lake in The Kingdom of the Owls, never approaching, just observing.

The Way of the Aves is bent by the Order, who defile it to their own gains, his mind told him, showing the Sparrows flying under the moonlight, carrying torches as bright as the sun.

They judge. They judge, they judge, they judge, his mind kept on saying. At each repetition, an ave appeared. First, it was the ones by the Lake in the Kingdom of the Owls. Then, the Mountain Eagles, who'd attacked him before even asking who he was appeared, followed by Lord Reemus and the council.

This Land needs to burn. This way needs to burn. Everyone must pay for it, and all needs to be remade. A new world should be ushered in, his mind told him, making Raven feel thirsty, bringing back the feeling he'd had as he crossed the mountain.

Inside the dark void of his mind, he saw a stream passing by, locked behind walls he needed to break. In reality, he was charging out of control towards the ceiling.

Let's use my rightful powers to sink this place and end this conflict once and for all. This time, the thought happened in reality.

Two female vultures rushed past the Sparrow knights, who allowed them passage purposefully. In front of Stragif were the five vultures born by the sinful union.

Now, this tale finally ends. No family will be treated differently anymore. A bitter thought but a necessary one in Stragif's mind.

"In the end, you came to our side," Zephyr smugly observed, looking at Zola.

"Feelings aside, you're all still family to me," Zola replied.

Dexter glided down right next to Stragif, startling him for a second. "I managed to find both your daughters and leave them by the exit," he reported, "but I still have seen no sign of your wife."

"The Creator surely is watching over her, woo," Stragif said, letting a relieved sigh escape him. "Let's take this opportunity Raven gave us and finish these monsters off, woo. When everything has calmed down, we can find my dear Griphi."

Dexter nodded to George, who, in reply, raised his wings upwards, giving the remaining Sparrow soldiers the command to end this once and for all.

"We won't go down without a fight," Zephyr shouted at them.

"Don't let them taint you, soldiers," Dexter said with an imposing tone. "I saw with my own eyes that those savage beasts can't fly here. The female vulture couldn't keep a hold of her own weight. In the Creator's forsaken cave, we are the masters of the wind."

Everlasting light, brilliant and eternal, emerged from Raven. Stragif couldn't do much, he had to look at it.

"Is he moving away from us?" he heard George asking. He, too, had noticed the light getting dimmer and dimmer as the synthetic sun rose up.

The sun collided with the ceiling above, and small cracks spidered from the epicenter of the impact. From the ruptures, hydra slowly began to pour down. Raven collided against it again, the cracks enlarging with every hit.

"He dares to drown us all!" a sparrow knight exclaimed as a pillar of water fell from the ceiling and washed everyone away.

Creator be damned! Raven will kill all the vultures this way, but Griphi— She is still missing. I need to stop him, Stragif thought, his heart racing.

"Dexter, please, take me to Raven. I can't fly here properly, but you surely can," Stragif demanded of him. Dexter obeyed without hesitation.

"Don't let the vultures move," George commanded his fellow soldiers. Even as the sea hydra quickly started to rise, the soldiers bravely moved in circles around the vultures, poking them from time to time to keep them in their place. The hydra added an extra layer of difficulty to moving, and for creatures their size who were born to fly, the situation was dire. None of them were swans, capable of floating above the water with ease, especially not water flowing at such high speed.

Stragif climbed towards the cave's ceiling on Dexter's back. He scanned the ground below, trying to find his wife, but Raven's new location dimmed the light below, and the dense vegetation clouded his vision.

And then, he and Raven were face-to-face. Stragif didn't dare to look at him, the brightness of Raven's rainbow flames would burn his vision in seconds.

"I can't stay here. My armor is melting. You'll have to do the rest. I'll look for your wife while you do," Dexter said, leaving Stragif to glide next to Raven. Being at the center of the storm, where the air was calmer, allowed him to do so with ease.

"My friend, woo, don't you see what you're doing? You're going to kill us all, my wife included." Stragif said. The "woo," this time, came out forced, as if he was trying to sound like his calm and friendly persona.

Raven didn't listen. Instead, he rushed upward again, colliding against the ceiling. New waterfalls emerged from the ever-growing number of cracks.

"I know you're mad, woo. I, too, want the vultures dead for good. I—"

Stragif's feathers burned, for Raven suddenly caught him, holding him tight between his wings.

"How *dare* you talk to me! I would never wish to have Zola killed," Raven spoke; his voice was rough and deep, as if he wasn't himself. His feathers' flames ceased, allowing Stragif to rest easy, but Raven's thoughts still burned with rage.

"But, Raven, don't you see? The vultures threatened my family twice, hunted you, killed many Aves across the Land, and their existence brought confusion regarding your identity," Stragif said, trying to escape from Raven's clasp but failing. Raven, somehow, was far stronger than when they first met. "Killing them would end all of this. It would end the betrayal Lord Corvax announced when he threatened the Phoenixes. We can put an end to this, once and for all," he pleaded. No matter how much he tried, no "woo" could leave his beak. He was far too nervous for that.

"You *dare* to talk about betrayal when you led me and my… my… partner to this trap! You're the betrayer here!" Raven spat with disdain.

"But, Raven—"

"*Lord* Raven! This is how you shall address me from here on out, traitor."

"Raven, I—"

"I told you to call me 'Lord'! You shall be the first to do so but not the last. The Land will be reborn under my wings. The era of Starlight and Sunshine will be over, and the Orders shall crumble."

"Please, my friend, you can't be serious," Stragif said, terrified.

"She died by losing a wing, didn't she?" Raven asked, clearly not expecting an answer.

"Died? You mea—"

Raven's beak plunged into Stragif's left wing. The peck went deep into his flesh.

"A wing for a wing," Stragif heard Raven trying to say as his beak moved back and forth. The flames in Raven's body ignited once again.

Stragif screamed as his left wing was completely removed from his body in one brutal movement. The entire cave fell silent. No one watching the scene could say a single word. Even the hydra seemed to cry.

"As a punishment, you shall never fly again," Raven proclaimed, the flames dimming once again, but his eyes were still bright with fury. "Now, do it. Be the first to call me 'Lord Raven,'" Raven slowly ordered.

"Lord… Raven…" Stragif said in pain.

And then, he fell from far above, motionless, just like Zola did.

Time to finish this, once and for all. The rebellion begins here, Raven told himself. His body was shining brighter than the sun. He was a new star.

With all his might, he hit the cave's ceiling and destroyed it once and for all. Sea hydra poured down like a beaver's dam had been destroyed, flooding the area in front of it.

Raven felt satisfied; no one would leave the cave. Then, from above, he saw it: a small, purple, bioluminescent structure moving in the water.

Zola's necklace. I might as well take it and see if I can find her body, Raven thought, diving deep into the newly formed lake. Strong currents moved everything left and right towards the passages leading to where Mount Kingdom Come was supposed to be. Raven didn't care about that. He followed the reef that acted like a beacon of his dearly parted lover. To his surprise, when he saw her body, her eyes were wide open and panicked-looking. A bubble of air was made under Raven's command, protecting Zola.

"Raven, where is my family?" Zola asked between deep coughs.

The hydra came to a full stop. "Is that what you wish? For me to save them? My dear, tell me. I thought I'd lost you. I don't want you thinking you lost them."

"Yes, please," she said, almost collapsing. Her wounds were open again.

"It shall be done," Raven said, and he commanded the current to carry her to the cave's entrance.

He searched the hydra and all the bodies floating in it, but he couldn't precisely locate her family. *My powers aren't so precise,* he thought, giving the hydra a new command: *You shall flow and take each body out, dead or alive.* The flow of hydra became chaotic, so Raven flew away, exiting it. From above, the chaos formed what seemed like a living organism to him, but it lacked any order. Order was something Raven wanted gone.

Bodies could be seen floating out. He saw Stragif, the Sparrow knights, and even Griphi. After a while, he spotted all the vultures, left alone in a different section of the cave, away from the Sparrows so that they could escape.

Raven flew back out of the cave. At the entrance, he saw Morpha and Phorma hugging each other in tears. He passed over them without saying a single word.

"It's done. Your family is safe. Rest assured, if they do no harm to me or you, that shall remain the case," Raven told Zola.

"Thank you," Zola said. "Where are we going now?"

"We'll hide until you get stronger. Then, we shall change the Land itself."

"I'm sorry, Raven. I hope this isn't all my fault," Zola told him, collapsing once and for all. Thankfully, Raven had, by then, found the strength to order the wind to help him carry her.

Murdek was disappearing from the horizon, Delmartica would soon take its place, and the day-and-night cycle would continue as ordained by the Creator.

"'I'm sorry,' huh?" Raven said as if Zola could listen. "In the future that I'll create, you won't need to apologize anymore."

Epilogue

I thought the day was over. The sun had surely set, and yet, in the middle of the dark sky, something shone brighter than any star. It was Murdek, which, from time to time, would be burning with fire.

"It seems Raven's conquest continues to be challenged," I told the Golden Egg that still slept in the highest tower of Fort Gallus. "I heard multiple tales, whispers from the secret Aves that seek to invade Delmartica next," I continued.

"Lord Melchizedek." One of my most trusted Roost rushed in with a parchment in his hand. "I have a message from afar. Dwighticus seems to request information regarding Devonaire," he told me, passing the parchment over.

I glanced over it. Each letter told me more and more about the drastic state of the Land, reassuring me of my position. I waved, requesting the guard to leave.

"It seems the time has come for me to tell you the reason you're here," I told the Golden Egg. "It seems Sunshine and the JuJuRana are of the same mind as mine: You need to hear the stories before your birth; otherwise, it might be too late for your destiny to be fulfilled."

I sat by its side. The braziers in the room burned bright, and each flame flickered, pointing in a single direction, venerating the Golden Egg. The tower allowed it to be far above the Land—a decision I made, for we needed it to be touched by sunlight from time to time—and yet, the soil rose to greet him time and time again. Rocks grew from the underground, and others used the winds to invade the room in search of their rightful master.

"Well, this tale is a special one for, unlike any other, the Order of the Owls never managed to write it down. A secret spot in the long, detailed, recorded history we so proudly have now—one that, in the future, we will be as incapable of understanding as the ruined settlements from the days before the Dark Years," I told him.

"It all began with the fall of Murdek. The overthrow that happened there was brutal, and despite all the bloodshed, Raven wasn't satisfied. He aimed for Delmartica, leading Sunshine, the Golden Phoenix, Protector of the Sun, and Harrier of the Cycle of the Day, to take a drastic action: to deliver you into my care.

"You see, little one, the Creator, in all his grace and glory, created two powerful eggs: one for each inhabitant of the sacred lands of Murdek and Delmartica. The Silver Egg was meant to hatch and bring forth the God of the Night, his partner being Starlight, the Guardian of the Moon. From this one, Raven was born.

"The second egg was golden in nature, stored in Delmartica, and from it, the God of the Day was to be born, and together with his future partner Sunshine, the Guardian of the Sun, the Golden Phoenix would lead the day. From this egg, Dwighticus was born. By now, you might be wondering about yourself. Well, you were laid later. A tremendous boom could be heard in Delmartica when you came into being, or so I heard.

"In the days following the conquering of Murdek, a bridge between the heavens and the firmament opened, revealing to me a secret many don't know: Mount Kingdom Come isn't the only location on the Land that the goddesses can use to travel and communicate. This is just a theory, mind you, but I believe that many of those passages are hidden around. Otherwise, the only explanation I can conjure is that the Phoenixes can travel anytime they want, and Raven was just never taught about such an interesting power. Had he been, maybe all of this could have been prevented…"

I lost my train of thought for a moment, and my wings moved over my wattle as I tried to think of what could be if such knowledge was readily available to Raven from the get-go. But to think in such terms is usually a waste of time. What has come and gone cannot be changed; time cannot be undone. Doing so would be meaningless, much like chasing the wind.

"Apologies, little one. I hope you'll forgive this old rooster's thoughts and ramblings. But well, where was I again? Oh yes, the Sun found a way to reach the Land without burning it: the bridge that, if my mind recalls, was nothing more than a tunnel in the void, invisible to those who didn't know where to look. The dust and the clouds touched and bent around it, revealing the trick easily. It was a corridor by another name.

"Flying down within it was Sunshine. Her golden flames almost burned the Kingdom of the Roosters to a crisp, so she remained afloat as far as she could. A different Phoenix was capable of approaching us, however. His flames were golden, just like our beautiful harrier of the day, but tamer. Dwighticus was his name. In his hands, he carried a golden egg. An egg that, as soon as it left the bridge, drew the flames of the world towards it. The Land created rumors that it was Raven's doing by manipulating the wind. But the truth is quite simple. It was you arriving, being greeted by what is rightfully yours to command."

"'Please,' I heard Dwighticus say, 'Lord Melchizedek, Raven surely aims to destroy Delmartica. This egg must never reach his hands, no matter what,'" I pretended to be the JuJuRana by changing my voice to a rough-sounding one. Hatchlings tended to like it when I impersonated others in my story.

"Of course," I proudly answered, both back in the day and then in my simple performance. To add a gravitas, I stood up and pretended to be talking with Dwighticus. The Golden Egg couldn't see it, I knew that, but still, what if he could? Once, we believed Mount Kingdom Come was the only way to reach the heavens, but we were proven wrong, so I continued my performance, just in case. "The Order of Gallus and, more importantly, the Family of the Fighting Rooster serves the Way of the Aves and the Creator's Laws. What must be done shall be done," I said as myself.

"We, the JuJuRana, appreciate such devotion," I intoned as Dwighticus. "The egg shall be kept down here in secret and raised on the Land while a hatchling. Your Family and Order will guide him, teach him all he needs to know, and nurture his needs and wants. I am requesting that there are murals of the history of the Land painted wherever you'll keep him so he can learn about the events that led us to take such actions and be prevented from becoming another Raven."

"We surely can do all of that, sir," I said, changing back to my own self. "But if you don't mind me asking, why is this egg so important?"

"This egg represents a threat to Raven's domain," Starlight said as she continued her descent from the heavens. To this day, I don't know where she came from or where she went after. "His war against the heavens requires knowledge, strength, and wisdom. We believe, if our bets are right, the JuJuRana that shall hatch from this egg will bring forth the end of Exodus," I said with the highest-pitched voice I could manage, pretending to fly around the room. In all fairness, Starlight's voice was far deeper and stronger than my impression implied.

"This explanation shall suffice," I embraced my own persona once again. "Me and my Order will protect this egg till the end of time if needs be."

"'Thank you for all the help provided,' Sunshine said from far away. My skin and feathers felt a warmth coming from her, even across such a distance. 'Could I please ask for a single, simple thing? I care deeply for this egg. Me and the JuJuRana would love to know of his fate on a daily basis. Would you please signal us in some manner so that we know the Path to the Exodus is still distant, and the fight is still ongoing? Please, I beg of you.' And I said yes of course," I told the little egg, ending the theater, noticing the night was almost over. The egg trembled a bit, and my heart almost went wild. But it was only for a moment; the Golden Egg did not respond after.

"You're such a good spectator, always quiet when needed, and I can hear the applause coming with a simple shaking. I can't wait to meet you, a name has even been provided. Sorry, I skipped that part of the dialogue," I told him, laughing a little. "You shall be called Devonaire."

"Fear. Faith. Love. This is the true Cycle of Life," I spoke, the words etching themselves in the air, for they were the foundation of all things after all. I left the room where the egg remained, setting my feet on the open wilds. Fort Gallus had grown in the past few years; walls towered over everything, removing parts of the vegetation that once we ignored and giving rise to a corn farm with a military compound hidden within. We did this out of Fear.

But we had knowledge provided by our elders. In this instance, the JuJuRana, Starlight, and the history of how they ended the Dark Years of Madness, gave us faith that they knew how to end the rebellion Raven had started. Faith in our Elders guided us.

And where there is Faith, there is hope for better days—hope that the future matters and that we will be capable of flying towards it. Once one decides to fly to the future, I have found that they also want to leave the seed of their presence in the world—leaving Aves of their own. And for that, they need Love—a natural reaction.

Raven found love amidst fear and rage. Was that always intended? Does he have Faith in Zola? Those questions circled in my head day and night, especially after reading *The Rainbow Hunter* by Stragif, the flightless Owl. In his writings, he mentioned Raven noticing Love for the first time while they crossed the mountains. Did Raven fail to see the Faith the two lovers also felt? Or was it Faith in himself and in Zola that led him to take so many drastic measures?

I walked to the top of the second-highest tower in all of Fort Gallus, with openings facing east. From there, I wondered more and more about the events that had allowed me to be here, as I watched a burning Murdek vanish from the horizon, announcing the end of the night.

It was time for me to deliver the daily message to Sunshine and the JuJuRana, reassuring them that the Exodus remained at bay. I took a deep breath, inhaling as much air as I could. Then, I prepared to exhale it, singing a song that could be heard across the whole Land and beyond.

"Cock-a-doodle-doo."

The morning had risen, and the Land remained safe.

About the Author

TD Dickinson brings a unique blend of experience to her current studies. A retired U.S. Air Force veteran with an Associate's degree in Meteorology, she is now pursuing a Bachelor's degree in Fashion Merchandising and Branding at Stevens – The Institute for Business and Art. Her life balances academic pursuits with strong family and faith ties. A devoted mother to Mekia, Malachi, and Matthias, and a loving owner of her dog, Bella Mae, she also actively participates in her family's business and volunteers at Great Commission Lutheran Church in St. Louis, where her father is the pastor. Her spiritual foundation is deeply rooted in her upbringing in Clarke County, Mississippi, at New Fellowship Missionary Baptist Church.

Beyond her professional and family commitments, Dickinson cultivates a rich and diverse personal life. Her interests span a wide range of creative and introspective activities. She enjoys reading, meditation, and yoga, as well as more hands-on hobbies like DIY crafting and designing her own clothes. Music is a significant part of her life, with singing and playing multiple instruments, including the piano.